Windstorm

Windstorm

Ted Simmons

Tallahassee, Florida

© 2010 by Ted Simmons

Cover art © 2010 by Mark Simmons

All rights reserved. No part of this book may be reproduced in any form or by any means, electronic or mechanical, including photocopying, recording, or by any information storage and retrieval system, without permission in writing from the publisher, except for brief quotations contained in critical articles and reviews.

Inquiries should be addressed to:
CyPress Publications
P.O. Box 2636
Tallahassee, Florida 32316-2636
http://cypresspublications.com
lraymond@nettally.com

ISBN: 978-1-935083-13-9
First Edition

Dedication

*For Judy Gross and Louise Kahn
whose warm support and wise advice
have been the foundation
on which this and all my works reside*

Chapter 1

London, England, March 1982

THE NORTHBOUND PLATFORM AT St. John's Wood Station was eerily deserted. Carter stood alone, staring at the concrete floor and absently scuffing his brand new Nikes on the grimy surface. His body wasn't moving, but his mind was flipping back and forth like crazy. He kept thinking of the friends he'd left behind in what was already starting to feel like an old movie. Tom, Daniel, Sandy. Oh yes, Sandy. For the first time in his life he'd worked up the courage to ask a girl out on an honest-to-God date, and it looked like it might turn into a long-term thing. Then Dad came home and dropped his bombshell. Tom, Daniel, and Sandy were now five thousand miles away and only lived in the movie inside his head.

Alone on the platform, Carter forced his mind back to the present. He'd stayed over at school a couple of hours to work with Mr. Graham, his home room teacher, on make-up assignments. He was way, way behind his classmates because the transfer to ASL was in mid-term. Actually, not even mid-term, because the summer break was just two weeks away. All his new classmates were cramming for finals in courses he hadn't even taken. What a crock this was. *Thanks, Dad.*

The American School in London was in a quiet suburb, where there weren't many factories or offices or things like that, so not many people got on the outbound train. Except for students like him. And, thanks to his late departure, he was the only one there. The platform was dead quiet—but just for a minute.

When the train rolled in, he could hear the din while the cars were still moving and before the doors opened. When they did, the noise swept out like a violent storm. Shouting and cussing and off-key singing. Inside the train, he could see women and older people cowering in their seats, while the aisles were filled to capacity with pushing, shoving young men and boys, most not much older than his seventeen years. *Sheesh,* he thought, *I've run into rowdy kids before, but nothing like this.*

He ran along the platform searching for the least crowded car. His backpack flumped up and down, extra-loaded with a gazillion books that needed his attention. Then the doors started to close, and he had no choice but to leap through the closest one, hoping those gazillion books didn't get caught on the outside. The force of his charge brought him up against the back of a guy in a green windbreaker who was just winding up to slug someone in front of him. He missed and fell forward, and the one he was trying to hit took a swipe at the side of his head. Down he went. A dozen voices quit cussing and singing and started to laugh.

Carter wasn't one of them. As the train lurched forward and then rolled smoothly out of the station, he watched green windbreaker grab onto the silver pole people use to steady themselves. He was having trouble hauling himself up. It was crazy, Carter thought, but through all that, the guy was still clutching a can of beer to his chest with his left hand. He looked pretty smashed. When the fellow who'd knocked him down reached over and tried to help him stand, Carter knew he was in trouble. These were guys who got off on beating the crap out of each other and then ending up hugging and singing. He figured this guy wouldn't hesitate to beat the crap out of a stranger. No singing involved.

He tried to edge himself through the crowd, hoping to get out of sight, and hopefully out of mind, of green windbreaker. But the raucous, already-plastered-at-five-p.m. crowd wouldn't let him through.

"Lookie here. Whatcha got there, ya skinny poofter?"

Someone started to pull open his backpack. He jerked away. "Oooh, lotsa books, huh?"

"He got on at St. John's Wood. Gotta be one a them Yank swots."

"Whyn'tcha say something, Yank? Stand their with yer cake-hole open."

He tried to pull himself together and act as stoic as possible. He'd met enough bullies to know if he showed weakness, they'd be all over him.

"So who are you guys?" he said. "You all just break out of jail or something?"

It seemed like the right thing to say, because everyone around him started laughing again. One next to Carter threw his arm over his shoulder, leaned in and said, in a beer-drenched voice, "You said it, chum, so look out, ladies, we're randy as hell."

"Look out, skinny poofters, too!"

Green windbreaker was fully upright and lurching toward Carter. Just then, the train started to brake for the next station. All the inebriated louts standing in the aisle stumbled forward, and windbreaker grabbed the pole with both hands, losing his beer in the process. When the doors opened he was back down on his knees, groping for the can and swearing like a drunken pirate. Carter slipped by him and out the door.

On the platform he ran toward the back of the train and went into another car, this time with a little more finesse. It was just as crowded, but at least here he hadn't made such a grand entrance. He worked his way toward the back, nodding his head in time to what he assumed was some sort of soccer football club song. He hoped he looked like just one of the lads.

Then his new-found sense of comfort got stripped away. In fact, he stripped it away himself. In his new surroundings, Carter Chamberlain wasn't the one getting picked on. It was a girl. Red-brown-haired, about his age. She was probably pretty, but her face was all screwed up in what he could only describe as half fear, half anger. He could see she could probably hold her own in any one-on-one situation, but this was too much. She was totally surrounded by leering, cursing, drunken louts, who were poking at her breasts and pulling at her hair.

He couldn't stand and watch this. He knew it was probably stupid to get involved, but he was still on an adrenaline high from his adventure in the other car, so he just plowed in and started to throw punches at her tormentors. Most of them missed, but some didn't, and he found himself the target of far more angry fists than he was giving out. Luckily, this bunch was every bit as drunk as the guys in the other car, and most of the fists whizzed by him completely. Then, either by accident or on purpose, they started slugging each other, and Carter was in the middle of an old western barroom brawl. He grabbed the girl and pulled her up against the door that goes into the next car, and they sank down on the floor, out of range of the fistfight raging above.

She started to pull away, but then she grabbed on and clung to him. They stayed that way until the train reached the next station. Somebody shouted, "Wembley, mates!" and the fighting stopped like magic. Nearly the whole crowd cheered and lurched to the door and out onto the platform, elbowing and shoving. Outside, they started in with the off-key singing, as they staggered toward the exit.

There were maybe a dozen people left in the train car. Some were business types, gripping their briefcases like they were filled with the Queen's jewels. Two were women who'd obviously been in town shopping. They were hunched over, hugging their day's acquisitions. One was an older woman who clutched her hands together to her throat. Her face was almost as white as her hair, and Carter suspected she'd looked a lot younger a few minutes earlier.

Then there was him. And the girl who was clinging to him like a winter coat. He didn't know what to do. Normally, he'd have gotten off at Wembley Park Station himself, to change to an express train that went straight through to Rickmansworth, where he lived. But he wasn't about to do that this time, for two reasons. One, he wasn't about to get tangled up with the gang of soccer hoodlums that just got out. Second, he had a pretty, red-haired girl squeezing her arms around him and dripping big fat tears all over his chest.

Chapter 2

THE TRAIN HAD STOPPED AT TWO more stations before the girl pushed away, keeping her hands on his shoulders and staring into his face with a puzzled look on hers. He figured she was trying to decide whether he was the brave but stupid fellow he seemed to be, or just another guy trying to take advantage of the situation to take advantage of her.

He tried to disarm her by saying, "Hi, there."

She gave him a weak smile and wiped away some of her tears with the sleeve of her blouse. She kept her free hand on his shoulder. *She being friendly, or just making sure I keep my distance?*

"Hello there, y'rself," she said. Her voice was deeper than he would have expected—very Irish, very nice.

"I'm Carter Chamberlain," he blurted out. "I'm an American." *Jeez, Carter, what was that about? Now she thinks I'm an American dork.*

"I'm Fiona. And I could tell."

"Tell what?"

"That you're a Yank."

He shook his head. "No way. No way you can take one look at me and know I'm American."

"But I can, and I did."

He shrugged his backpack off his shoulders and held it in his lap. Fiona pointed to the backpack and said, "You're on your way home from school. You're wearing jeans and a striped shirt, not a uniform, so—you're American. Simple, really."

"All right. My turn. I can take one look at you and say . . ." He tilted his head and studied her. ". . . you must be . . . Irish!"

"Silly." She slugged his shoulder. "I've got an Irish name, and I talk with a Dublin brogue . . . so I'm told."

"Well, that helped, too. A little bit."

"Don't ya think maybe the two of us could get off the floor and sit properly in the seats?"

"Sure." He leaped up, dumping his backpack. Several books fell out and skittered away. He tried to intercept them with one toe, to keep them from sliding under the seats. At the same time he was bending down to help Fiona to her feet. He didn't do a very good job of either, but, finally, Fiona was sitting and he was back on the floor, searching for wayward reading material. Not his finest hour.

He tried to steer the conversation away from himself. "So who were those bozos in here, drunk in the middle of the afternoon?"

"Typical. England's playing Germany or someone at Wembley Stadium."

"Ah. So those were the famous British football hooligans?"

"Oh yes. Just think how welcome the lads are when they go to Germany or, heaven help us, France."

They sat on a bench seat facing sideways. No one was in the opposite seats across the aisle, so they had a panoramic view of London suburbs flashing by. Clusters of dense housing and shops, with a few green spaces here and there. They were going through an area where the train was elevated, so they could see almost directly into the second-story windows of the row houses backing on to the track. Carter thought, if the Chamberlain family lived in one of those places, they'd have their blinds drawn tight, but a surprising number of these people had the curtains up and the windows wide open.

As they slowed for a station, Fiona pointed and said, "Oh, lookie there!" A semi-naked couple were in what appeared to be a kitchen. The man had the woman pressed back against a wooden table, trying to nip at her neck. Carter was embarrassed, but couldn't help but stare. He glanced over at his companion and saw she wasn't even slightly embarrassed. Go figure.

"Yer turnin' a bit red a the face," said Fiona.

"It must've been the fight," he said.

She chuckled. "Right. Musta been."

"How long have you lived in London?" he asked, trying to change the subject.

"A bit. And how about the Yank?"

"Two weeks. My dad just got transferred here." He pointed to his backpack, again in its place on his lap. "That's why I've got mounds of homework. Not fair, really. I didn't ask to get pulled outta my old school in the middle of the year. I was doing just fine, and now it's like I'm starting over."

Fiona shook her head. "Tssk, tssk. Poor boy."

He wanted to hide his face in his hands. *How can I keep saying these dumb-ass things? She must really wonder about me.* Time to change the subject again. "Do you have brothers and sisters?"

This seemed like a pretty innocuous question, but after he asked it she stared for the longest time at the floor. Finally, she said, "Two."

"Sisters?"

Fiona shook her head. "No! . . . both brothers. Two brothers, no sisters . . . and you?"

"Two. Both sisters. Two sisters, no brothers."

Fiona had been staring at the floor. She looked up and smiled for a millisecond, then looked back down, apparently interested in a bright yellow gum wrapper.

He tried again. "What do your parents do?"

This time her answer was immediate and hard. "Nothing. Me dad does nothing, on account of he's dead. Me mum does nothing, on account of she's total loopers. She looped out of it when he died, and she hasn't been with it since."

"Jeez. I'm sorry. How long's it been?"

Fiona got real quiet again. When she spoke, he could barely hear her. "A bit."

Now it was his turn to be quiet. He was trying to figure out why some things seemed to be off limits with this girl. She seemed to be a crazy mixture of toughness and vulnerability he'd never before seen in one person. He decided he needed to get to know her better. As an intellectual exercise, of course. Her shoulder-length auburn hair, the few tiny freckles on her nose, her oval face and her voice, her deep, sexy voice—none of these things mattered, of course. And the fact he'd developed a pressing need to keep his backpack planted firmly in his lap—that didn't matter, either. She was pure and simple a mystery that needed to be solved.

They were pulling in to what he was pretty sure was the last station before his, which was the end of the line for this train. He was hoping she'd be getting off at Rickmansworth with him, but she must have read his mind. She was shaking her head slightly and said, "Northwood. My stop, Northwood."

She was at the doors while they were still closed, and he shouted, "Wait. Can I see you again sometime?"

She turned and looked at him for a few seconds. "I don't think so." Then she gave Carter a sad, crooked smile that made him think her words hurt her as much as they did him. She turned sideways and slipped through the still-opening doors, and was gone.

I don't care what she said. I'll find her. She'll take those words back. I'll find her. But would he? In all his questioning of Fiona and her family, he hadn't found out one little detail. He didn't know her last name.

Chapter 3

WHEN THE TRAIN PULLED IN TO the Rickmansworth Station, Carter was mulling around the question of finding Fiona, when he realized someone was staring at him. It was the old lady he'd seen clutching her throat in apparent terror earlier. She didn't appear terrified anymore. In fact, she was smiling. He smiled back, wondering what it was about him that attracted her attention. He tried to picture how he might appear to a stranger, and came up with the one-word description, "ordinary." Dark brown hair, a touch longer than his dad likes, a six-foot body a touch skinnier than *he'd* like, a chin that wasn't square or pointy or missing, a face that was neither pasty or tanned, or anything other than—ordinary. So what was the old lady smiling at?

They stood next to each other at the door. She was still beaming at him and nodding her head. When the doors fully opened, Carter got off quickly and then extended his hand to help her down. On the platform, she turned toward him fully and said, "My, how refreshing to encounter a real gentleman."

Carter stammered a bit, but managed to say, "Yes, ma'am," or something that sounded lame even before it cleared his throat.

She didn't seem to notice his embarrassment. "That was quite an interesting journey, wasn't it?"

"Uh huh, interesting."

"I try to avoid traveling before football games at Wembley."

"Yes, ma'am."

She transferred her shopping bag to her left hand and put her right hand on Carter's shoulder. He felt another flush pass over him, similar to what he'd just experienced with Fiona, but this time it was confined to his face.

"My girlfriends and I would love to have you join us for a pint, sometimes." She pointed toward a nearby pub, the *Cock and Crow*. "We rarely have the privilege of entertaining a true gentleman, at least not one of your generation."

"I . . . I . . . I don't think . . . I mean, I don't really drink. I'm just . . ."

"Nonsense, my boy. Everybody drinks something."

"*Some* people drink more than something." Carter realized his voice had turned hard. He cocked his head and gave the old lady what he hoped was a disarming smile and added, "Sometimes."

Apparently she hadn't noticed his brief change of mood, because she kept her free hand on his shoulder while they walked across the parking lot and maintained a steady stream of chatter. After a while Carter did actually find himself getting interested in her stories about the local eccentrics, and was happy enough to give her a story about his "incredibly dull life" and his "incredibly dull family." She ate it up like he was delivering a state-of-the-union speech.

When they parted company, she went left and Carter went right, across the street toward home. He looked back at the same time as the old lady, and she waved at him. He waved back and then had an unsettling thought. He hadn't learned her name! First Fiona and now the lady. *What an idiot, Carter. Twice in less than an hour.* His only consolation came when he realized the old lady hadn't asked for his name, either.

As he trudged up the path to his house, Carter Chamberlain replayed everything that had happened between St. John's Wood and home. The minute he walked in, though, and saw his mother splayed out in an easy chair, heavy-lidded eyes glued to the television, these thoughts disappeared in a flash. He sat down quietly next to her and rescued a glass of something brown she'd let tip to a forty-five-degree angle. She didn't seem to notice her son or the loss of the glass. She was caught up in what the announcer said was, "breaking news from downtown London." The scene of carnage on the screen was so bad it seemed unreal. Something out of Hollywood. Carter thought briefly about how terrible it was for the people involved and their families, but heck, they weren't really real, just images on a screen. He put his arm around his mother, and she absently took his hand. *How lucky I am really. How good it is to have a family to love and a home to be safe in.* He said, "Hi, Mom. What can I fix for dinner?"

Chapter 4

THE BRICKWORK WAS STREAKED WITH black on black, suggesting it hadn't been cleaned since the days when London's East Enders derived their meager warmth from coal. The alleyway was devoid of light, too, and the dark figure who rapped tentatively at the grimy door would have been almost invisible to passersby in nearby Brixton Road. That was fine by him. Invisible was right good.

When no one responded, he knocked a tad louder, then cast his eyes about, nervously searching for anyone who might have heard him. All he saw was darkness, and all he heard was furtive scurrying behind the rubbish bins. It all seemed appropriate to his mission. Finally, he heard a muffled voice behind the door and rapped again, this time in the pattern that had been specified—three knocks, pause, three more. The door opened a crack, and he heard, "Who's this, then?"

By then, his nervousness had been replaced by impatience. "Crikey. Who'd ya think it was? It's Fergus, ya nit."

The door swung open then, and he was pulled roughly inside. The door thudded heavily behind him, and a bolt was shot.

"Did ya bring it?"

"Nah. I dinna. He weren't there."

"So why didn't ya wait on him? You know we needs those caps. Our work depends on those caps, and you was supposed to bring 'em."

"His flat was locked. After I pounded and shouted like a madman, the woman next door come out and told me he'd off and left. For Belgium or Belgravia or somewheres, she wasn't sure where. I asked her, 'Belfast, p'rhaps?' and she says maybe that could be it. Maybe not."

"Jaysus. Is he supposed to be comin' back?"

"The woman said, to be sure, he was comin' back. He'd better, 'cause she was supposed to go over every day and feed Kildare, that's 'is cat, and while she was happy enough to do that, she wasn't at all looking forward to cleaning out his litter . . . ."

"Good God, Fergus, spare me the catshit stories and gimme the bottom line here. Does he get back in time, or do we hafta find another source?"

"I . . . I . . . I dunno. The woman dinna know, so how . . ."

"Two weeks. We got two weeks. Our people is depending on us. The whole frickin' *cause* is depending on us."

"I know that. So whatta we do now?"

"Get everyone together. We gotta come up with a backup plan, and we gotta do it quick."

"My house, like last time?"

"Your sister away again?"

"Naah. She's home."

"Then where do you think we gotta meet? You daft or something? Bring everybody here. Night after tomorrow. After dark, same time. And, Fergus, if your nosy sister wants to know where you're goin', tell her you and Gordie's off to choir practice."

"We don't sing in no choir."

"Then make up one. Make up anything. How in hell did our glorious cause come to depend on little plonkers like you?"

Chapter 5

For the next few days, Carter was so busy trying to get himself up to speed in school, he had little time to think of Fiona what's-her-name, or the little old lady who wanted to share a pint with him, or even the continuing bad news on the telly.

The IRA, the Irish Republican Army, had started a fresh round of terrorist bombings aimed at British targets. Carter wasn't quite sure what their beef was. It had something to do with a place called Belfast, which was in a place called Northern Ireland, which he gathered the British and the Irish were fighting over, for some reason.

In the morning mail, the morning "post" they called it, there was a letter addressed to "Master Carter Chamberlain" in light purple ink. Sandy! When Carter recognized Sandy's handwriting, he felt a quick flash of guilt over the attention his mind and body had given the elusive Fiona, but then he started to wonder how Sandy knew where to address the letter. He figured maybe his dad had talked to someone in Houston by phone, and the word just spread.

Dear Carter,

I knew you would probably hear it from somebody else, so I decided to tell you myself, since I really do care about you. I've been cast in the school play in a leading role, and I'm so excited about it. You remember Matt Wilton, don't you? Anyway, he was cast opposite me, so we've been spending lots of time together rehearsing

and all, and we just kind of hit it off. Anyway, just thought you'd like to know I'm really happy. Hope you are, too.
    Sandy

    Two weeks. *Less* than two weeks, and Sandy had moved on and she was *happy*. She'd sent a letter halfway around the world—a *one*-short-paragraph letter. Carter sat at the blue Formica kitchen table and slowly tore the purple letter into little strips. Then he tried to rip the little strips sideways and found he could only tear about ten at a time. The pieces still seemed too big, so he divided them into smaller groups and kept on tearing until there was a small heap in the center of the table. When he tried to carry the pile to the waste bin under the sink, small white and purple flakes fluttered to the floor, and he had to get down on his hands and knees to sweep them up.
    "Whatcha doing?" Carter's younger sister Amy was standing in the doorway, pointing at him with something green on a stick.
    "Nothin'. Get the heck out of here. I'm busy."
    Amy didn't move. She knew from experience Carter's flashes of temper didn't last long, so she held her ground. She didn't say anything, though. It was part of the secret to handling her brother. If you just kept to yourself, he'd realize what a jerk he'd been and apologize. It didn't take long.
    "I'm sorry, Kitten." This was even better. When he used the nickname he'd given her when she was a baby, she knew he was *really* sorry for his outburst. "I just dropped some stuff, and I was trying to pick it up before Mom came in. She might be in one of her fussy moods today. You never know."
    "She might be in one of her not-noticing-anything moods, too."
    "Don't think so, Kitten. At least I hope not."
    "What's for dinner?"
    "I don't know. Want to help me? I think there's some hamburger meat in the freezer, and enough things to make spaghetti. That be all right for our Kitten?"

It was.

When the pasta was almost ready, Amy set the table for four. Even after half a year, Carter was conscious of the missing fifth setting that used to be occupied by his older sister Gwen, before she took herself off to college. He'd be ready for college himself in another year. Then who would cook the spaghetti?

Carter checked his watch. After six. Dad was late again. It seemed like it was turning into a normal thing, his being late. *Guess the new job takes getting used to.* When he went to the bedroom to fetch his mother, she shooed him away and said she needed to rest because of her headache.

From the kitchen doorway, he watched his little sister for a while, fussing over the placement of the napkins. When she noticed him, he said, "Guess what, Kitten. It's just the two of us for dinner. Why don't we put some pretty marigolds on the table and make it really, really special?"

Chapter 6

THE MEETING OFF THE BRIXTON ROAD alley had not been a peaceful one. Fergus and his brother were late because Gordie had a last minute emergency. A quick trip to the loo turned into a fifteen-minute event.

"What's goin' on, Gordo? You reading *Playboy* again?"

"Just feeling a bit sick a the stomach. I'll be okay in a sec."

"Too much a that cheap beer, kiddo. You oughta stick to the Guinness."

"Haven't had a thing. You know how Maddock gets if we ain't sharp when we're doing our planning."

"Screw Maddock . . . but you might wanta hurry, though."

Maddock was definitely in one of his moods when the brothers signaled their arrival with the furtive knock. He grabbed first Fergus and then Gordon and hauled them into the darkened room with such force, they ended up tangled in each other and some wooden chairs. He slammed the door hard and thrust the bolt home. Fergus wondered why all the noise, if they were trying to avoid being seen, or heard, by someone wandering through the alley. Maddock, Fergus thought, would have been perfect a thousand years ago driving the Norsemen into the sea at the Battle of Clontarf. But for this kind of secret, out-of-sight work, he was . . . well, anyway, he was the boss, and they had to go along with his tantrums. Maybe in a couple of weeks, when the job was done, they wouldn't have to put up with him anymore. All the more reason to get it done right, and get it over with.

"Where the hell you little pussies been? I been sittin' here forever waiting for you."

"I had to take a dump," said Gordon.

"A twenty-minute dump? You gotta be joking."

"Ease up on him, Maddock. He can't help it if he's got a gut-ache."

"He's a little pansy, and he's scared of the big time. Ain't that it, Gordie-boy?"

"It was a gut-ache. Nothin' more."

"And what about you, Fergus? I couldn't rely on you to get the story right about where Paddy'd gone," Maddock said. "So I went over there and had a nice chat with the catshit lady meself."

"And?"

"I told her I'd brought the dear little kitty some fresh meat, so she let me into Paddy's flat."

Fergus felt his low opinion of Maddock's abilities ease up a tad. "Find anything useful?"

"Found an address. Just a street, no town. But my guess is, it's Belfast all right. He'd scribbled the letters B.C. next to it."

"B.C. Don't mean nothing to me," said Fergus.

Gordon spoke up. "Blasting caps. B.C. means blasting caps." He looked for Maddock's reaction. "At least that's what it might be," he added weakly.

"'Course it does," said Maddock. "Anybody'd know that. So it looks like he went to Belfast to fetch 'em. So, Fergus, let's you and me get busy with the dynamite and the timer. Your job, little brother with the gut-ache, is to come up with something to put 'em in. Something the wankers in the park won't think don't belong."

"I thought we were goin' after military targets," said Gordon.

"Sure and we are, but if the soldier boys insist on parading around and showing off for them civilian idiots, we can't help if a few of the idiots get caught in the fun, too, now can we?"

"Guess not."

"Besides, if old John Q. Public gets blown up once in a while, they'll raise holy hell and insist their bloody government pull the bloody troops outta Northern Ireland. For us, it's all good. You feelin' good, Fergus?"

"Shite, yes."

"How about you, Gordo? How's the gut doing?"

"It's feeling good, Maddock, feeling good. I guess."

Chapter 7

Fiona McKenna was alternately overwhelmed with work or bored beyond belief. Either way, it was just short of unbearable. In quiet moments, she dreamed of being whisked away by some dashing young Sir Galahad, to a place where no one died and no one moaned in agony and no one spent all their days plotting terrible revenge. But then her mother's cry from the bedroom would bring her crashing back to the present. "Yes, Mother," she would say, trying to keep the exasperation out of her voice.

This evening was one of the quiet times. Mother was sleeping, or at least silent. Fergus and Gordie had left the house on one of their furtive missions. They claimed to be heading down to the pub for a few beers and some darts, but she knew better. Months before, she'd overheard a conversation between Fergus and an older man, a conversation that included "fireworks" and "teach the Limey bastards" and a few other choice words that told her something bad was in the works.

For years after their father's death, Fergus had stormed around, threatening revenge against the shadowy figures who'd sent a bullet into Durwin McKenna's brain, in full sight of his seventeen-year-old son. Then two years ago, Fergus had suddenly gone quiet. Fiona felt, knew absolutely, that Fergus's silence was more deadly than his violent rants. Something terrible was happening. And now, Gordie had been dragged into it. Gordie, the twin brother who'd been like an extension of herself, was now telling lies about beer and darts, and skulking off with Fergus. Fiona rubbed the tears off her cheeks. *Oh, hell.* Now even the quiet times were becoming unbearable.

Fiona leaned her head against the back of the couch and closed her eyes, squeezing out a few more tears. She didn't see the shape rising up from the floor, but felt two furry paws planted heavily on her breast and a raspy tongue on her cheek.

"Kerry Girl, that right hurts!" She pushed both white-tufted paws to the side, and Kerry Girl ended up crossways in Fiona's lap. The Sheltie had to twist her head almost backward to continue her attention to her mistress's face. Fiona couldn't help but laugh. Animals, she thought, have the most uncanny ability to sense when their humans are hurting, and the inclination to do something about it.

"Oh, girl, why can't we all be like you? You'd never, ever hurt the ones who love you, or tell them lies. Or live only to hate. Or . . ." Fiona stopped talking then, and hugged the brown-and-white bundle. Kerry Girl, having exhausted the supply of salty tears, hung her head and closed her eyes.

Fiona closed her eyes again, too, but now her thoughts moved away from her hate-filled brothers. She was envisioning another young man, the Yank on the train. Why he came to mind was a mystery. She stroked Kerry Girl behind the ears. *Maybe he reminds me of a puppy-dog. He did have that eager, friendly look to his eyes.* She tried to remember his name and finally came up with Carter, but the last name remained a blank. *Don't be daft, Fiona. You'll not see him again, and good thing, too.* There was no way she would open up her rotten life to a stranger, no matter how cute he was and how hard he might wag his tail.

Carter Chamberlain was enjoying a quiet moment, too. The all-too-short note from Sandy had hurt, sure, but in a strange way he felt relieved. Had he really expected Sandy to wait until he managed to get back to Houston? Had he really thought he'd be returning there any time soon? Or ever? If Sandy's letter had been filled with all kinds of mushy promises about saving herself for Carter and how she would be an empty shell until they were together—well, that meant Carter would have to make the same commitment. The truth was, their relationship had never progressed to the point where that made sense. It might have, in time, but their time had run out. Dad had seen to that.

There was one other reason Carter felt a permanent trans-Atlantic romance with Sandy was not such a hot idea. The surge of feeling he'd experienced for the mysterious girl on the train sure didn't fit with the need to act like a cloistered monk. Fiona. Fiona something-or-other. Fiona. Just saying the name made him feel a bit lightheaded.

Some detective work was definitely called for. The minute those awful final exams were over, he'd become a modern-day Sherlock Holmes. All he needed was a Watson to do his legwork and tell him how brilliant he was. He hadn't made many friends in London yet—hadn't had time, really. But there was one boy in his Chemistry class who would probably make a perfect sidekick for a world-class detective. Carter went to bed planning his recruiting campaign and envisioning how he and his partner-to-be would go about their detecting. Sleep was long in coming.

Fergus and Gordon McKenna decided to stop by the *Tethered Bull Pub* for a quick pint after all. That way, they could claim to have been there without lying. Gordie thought telling a lie was a pretty small crime compared to what they were planning to do, but Fergus would hear none of that. Fergus was of a mind to consider lying a sin, but blowing up people for a righteous cause was not. "You've gotta maintain a proper attitude, me lad. When the end is just, all the means is, too. Don'tcha forget that, boyo."

"I suppose. But isn't tellin' Fiona and Mum we've gone to the pub part of the means?"

"Suit yourself. If you want to sit there while I down me a jar, go ahead. Then you can lie your fool head off. Tell 'em you drank me under the table and beat me at darts, too."

"I suppose I could use a half-pint, anyway."

"Sure. Then you could just tell a half lie."

In the end, both Fergus and Gordon downed two full pints of lager before they realized time was slipping by and Maddock Lonigan would be fuming. Sure enough, when they'd been pulled in from the alley in the usual fashion, they were met with a stream of obscenities and a few choice punches to the chest.

"Don't tell me the both of you was holed up in the loo, holding your terrible sick stomachs. Chokin' the chickens more like it. Talk about brotherly love."

"We had to do something for our ma before we left. You want we shouldn't be good to our old lady?"

When Lonigan had calmed enough to turn his attention to their mission, he reported their missing compatriot had reported in, by telephone. Paddy O'Brien was in Belfast, Northern Ireland, all right, just as they'd suspected.

When Paddy'd rung up and announced himself, Maddock had tried to avoid shouting into the phone. He took a deep breath and said, "Sure but there musta been some place you might could've acquired some blasting caps closer to London, mate."

"Not without incurring a wee bit o' suspicion. Besides, I had me some personal business to attend to back home."

"Bollox! We've got ourselves a timetable here. Personal business should ought to wait."

When Maddock Lonigan recounted this conversation, he gave Fergus and Gordie a dark look to include them in his warning. Gordie paled and stared at his shoes. Fergus smiled a crooked smile.

"You think this is right funny? You think this is just a game?"

Fergus bristled. "Don't act like a total plonker, Lonigan. Tell me, which one of the two of us had his father murdered right in front of him by the goddam cowardly Ulster Volunteers? With the goddam British troops standing by to protect those friggin' Protestant bastards?"

"Okay, okay, Fergie. Calm down. What we're gonna do in less than two weeks is for you, for your auld mum, for your sister, even for Gordie, here. It's for your pa. Them goddam British troops who protected his murderers is gonna pay. And every last Englishman is gonna feel it."

Chapter 8

London's new Sherlock Holmes decided not to wait until after finals to recruit his Watson. They needed to be in a position to act immediately when summer break arrived. Come to think of it, this whole school thing seemed like total foolishness when there was important work to do. The original Sherlock never interrupted his detecting for anything as trivial as schoolwork.

"It's just a few miles away. Baker Street, where the great man lived. We could check it out during lunch hour."

Carter had decided to ease into his recruiting campaign. Instead of asking Josh Weaver to be his helper point-blank, he'd introduce Josh to things Sherlockian, then spring the proposal on him. Josh would be all primed and eager to accept. Elementary.

"Sorry, Carter. I'm really sweating exams this year. Can't take the time."

Carter didn't answer right away. His mind was racing to figure out what Sherlock would have done. Nothing came to mind. In all the stories, Holmes had already been Watson's boss, so there never was any question the junior man would do what he was told, even if the big guy kept him in the dark part of the time. No, it seemed like Carter Chamberlain was on his own for this one.

"What you need, Josh, is a study partner. You know, someone to go over old tests with you. Skim through your textbooks and drag out questions for you to answer. That sort of stuff."

"Aren't you, like, taking exams yourself?"

"Well, sure. But we got some of the same classes. When I help you, it's like you helpin' me. Besides, even though it's almost close enough to walk, we'd be taking the Underground train to Baker Street. We could study on the way. It'd hardly cost a minute."

They made their sojourn to the fabled detective's home the next day. According to the stories, he'd lived at 221B Baker Street. Only trouble was, they found there was no such place. There was a modern-looking building that had a bronze plaque on the front of it with a picture of Sherlock Holmes, but it sure didn't look like the kind of place that would have been around in the 1800s. It had another sign that said it belonged to the Abbey Road Building Society.

"I really don't have time to fool around, Carter," said Josh, giving his new friend a backward wave of his hand as he stalked off toward the Baker Street Tube Station.

"Wait. Wait. We've come all this way. Let's ask someone."

Josh agreed to give it a few minutes, which was a good thing, since one of the most important things for a detective to learn was patience, as well as the art of interviewing people. Carter realized, of course, Josh didn't know yet he was destined to become a famous detective's right-hand man. With Josh halfway upset about being dragged away from his stupid studying, it didn't seem like the right time to spring it on him. Carter told himself the original Sherlock would have said, "It appears not to be a propitious moment."

The first three people Carter stopped on the street gave him a curious look when he asked them about the Sherlock Holmes house. They just shook their heads and mumbled something foreign-sounding. Carter was beginning to wonder if there was anyone in the capital of the English-speaking world who spoke English.

Finally, he spotted an older man wearing a grey cap and a tweed jacket with leather patches on its elbows. He had a wind-chapped ruddy face and a nose that would have done Rudolph proud. When Carter asked him where he might find the Sherlock Holmes residence, the man cocked his head, nodded a couple of times, touched the tip of his finger to the red thing growing out of his face, and then pointed dramatically to the modern building beside them.

"Had there been," he said in a quivery voice, "had there been a 221B Baker Street, it would have been located at this very spot."

"Had there been?" said Carter.

"My dear lad, you do know that Sherlock Holmes was, in fact, a person of fiction, do you not? A creation of the fertile mind of one Sir Arthur Conan Doyle?"

Carter nodded.

"Furthermore, his place of abode was equally a work of fiction. In his early stories, he gave the address merely as 'Upper Baker Street,' and people believed he had in mind a place further along, near Regents Park."

"But then he gave it a number, 221B. There must have been . . ."

"Tut, tut, tut, lad. He gave it that number precisely because there was *no* actual property with that number."

"But why would he do that?"

"Oh, come, laddie. Think about it." With a smile and another nod of his head, the red-nosed man tipped his cap and strolled on.

On the way back to the train station, Carter was quiet and Josh was the one who seemed to want to talk. He said, "Not sure what you learned there. In fact, I don't have a clue what you wanted to learn. Why all this interest in some dead guy?"

"Not dead, fictional. There's a difference, Josh."

"Either way, he's not here, right? . . . So why are we here?"

"What'd you say?"

"I said, "Why are we here?"

"I can't talk about it right now," said Carter. "I've got some thinking to do."

Chapter 9

MADELEINE WESTFALL BROKE OUT laughing with such force, she spilled part of her pint of shandy before she had time to put it down, and the putting-down caused it to foam over even more. The mixture of beer and lemonade spread out on the dark wooden table, and she groped around through tear-filled eyes, searching for a napkin.

Her very dear friend, Crista Cordelia Piper, located a square of red-checked cloth and calmly wiped up the mess. She was the only one of the three companions who had total control of her emotions, because she was responsible for the uproar. A good comedian, she knew, never laughed at her own jokes. That privilege was reserved for the audience.

"Oh, C.C., that was wicked, just wicked." Beverly Kroome, the third party in the mid-afternoon gathering, was trying, unsuccessfully, to wipe away her own tears without smudging the generous amount of rouge on her cheeks.

"Oh, come now, Babs. I'm merely pointing out what everyone already knows. That size does matter. Men with large mustaches do make better lovers. It's a known fact."

Madeleine Westfall had recovered enough composure to rejoin the conversation. "I have heard, C.C., that *bald* men are the very best lovers. I've only heard, of course."

"Of course, Maddie. Of course."

"It appears the best of all worlds would be a bald man who *also* has a large mustache," said Beverly. Nods all around. "Much like that gorgeous young gentleman over there."

Madeleine Westfall and Crista Cordelia Piper both swiveled so quickly on their bar stools, they again spilled some of the afternoon's refreshment.

"Oh, I am so sorry, girls," said Beverly. "He ducked out into the sunlight. You must be getting old. You're much too slow."

"Hmmph. Speaking of gorgeous young men," said Crista Cordelia, "what became of your young American from the train, Maddie? You said you'd bring him around and introduce him to your two best friends. We are your best friends, are we not?"

"Sorry, girls. I haven't seen him since that one time. I know he lives hereabout, but I don't know where. Usually I'm busy avoiding the trains when he's coming home from school, it seems."

"Pity. From what you said, he seems a lovely boy."

"He was. Is. But what can I do?"

"You could sit outside the Rickmansworth Station and wait until he gets off a train."

"Right. People already think I'm a barmy old lady. What would they think then?"

"Tell them you're a sad, jilted housewife waiting for your two-timing husband who's gone off to London with his secretary."

"Then they'd be fawning all over me with, 'Oh, you poor dear. Oh, you precious old thing, you.'"

"Just tell them you've got a gun, and you're going to shoot the bastard. That would keep them away."

"It might keep people away, but the bobbies would haul *me* away. Smart."

"I'm just trying to help, Maddie."

"Why don't we take turns?" said Crista Cordelia.

"Doing what?"

"Waiting at the station. It'll be fun. And no one person will be there day-after-day looking strange."

"Why don't we all three wait?" said Beverly. "Together. Instead of meeting here at the *Cock and Crow,* we'll have our little parties on the platform at Rickmansworth Station."

"I don't think they serve proper beverages on the platform of the station," said Madeleine.

"We could hide our drinks in paper sacks, like the winos do."

"I thought the idea was not to look conspicuous. Three old broads drinking out of paper bags seems like it might be noticed. Just a tad."

Beverly laughed and said, "I think, for Maddie's sake, we could forego the liquid refreshment for a few days. Surely your young lad gets off the train every afternoon, don't you think?"

"I have some wizard lemon tortes I whipped up yesterday."

"Yeah, right, C.C., and I made a lovely plum pudding for the Queen."

"Well, I did buy them at Sainsbury's."

"If you all are so intent on helping me with my quest," said Madeleine, "I shall provide the refreshments."

"That's just smashing," said Crista Cordelia Piper.

"Just lovely," said Beverly Kroome.

"Just one thing," said Madeleine Westfall. "How do we avoid frightening the dear boy when three old crones leap on him when he gets off the train?"

Chapter 10

FIONA WAS ENGAGED IN A TRULY SPIRITED debate, a knock-down, drag-out fight where someone was going to be totally crushed. Unfortunately, that person was going to be Fiona McKenna, because she was debating herself. No matter which side won, she was bound to lose. She could either resign herself to a life of ongoing misery and stagnation, or she could take matters in hand and break out into what could be a life of troubles she couldn't even imagine.

What's more, she had in mind using a young man she didn't even know as the instrument to change her life. A boy, really, who she'd met only once and who'd probably forgotten she even existed. It truly was daft, she knew, but there was absolutely no one in the world, in her world anyway, who would be right for the job. Her loving brothers? They *were* the problem. Aunts, uncles, cousins? That lot had shown how close a family could be right after Pa's death. They'd melted away like snow on the Comeragh Mountains in July. How un-Irish is that?

She absently stroked Kerry Girl's underbelly, and the little Shetland Sheepdog squirmed in pleasure. It was ironic, really. Fiona's life had come down to this. Watching after a mother who demanded constant attention, and tending a small dog, a single small dog, in a world full of creatures who needed her. As far back as she could remember, she had vowed to devote her life to the care of animals. After a summertime visit to her Uncle Seamus's farmhouse near Connemara, a ten-year-old Fiona fell in love with horses. But just before the holiday ended, Bree, a small and gentle brown mare, stepped in a deep hole and fractured a leg. Her uncle hesitated less than a minute before placing a gun at Bree's temple. The little horse jerked left, and her hind legs collapsed. She tried valiantly to keep her front legs upright, but her eyes glazed and she fell to the side. Fiona heard Bree let out her last breath, a long drawn-out sigh, which sounded like wind in the trees.

Fiona's father explained there was no way to fix a terrible break like that, and Bree was best taken out of her pain. Fiona decided dogs and cats and rabbits could do without her help. She would devote her life to horses.

Fiona wasn't there a year later when, on a Belfast city street, another gunshot ended another life. She tried to imagine the scene, but everyone said she was too young to know the details. Fergus had been there, seen it all, but he told her to just shut her trap and "get off with ye" whenever she begged for answers. Among other things, she wondered if her father had sounded like the wind in the trees when he died.

Kerry Girl was oblivious to Fiona's mental time travel. She was a creature of the here and now. *A right good way to be.* The trouble with that, thought Fiona, was the here and now wasn't so cracker. The past was a skawly load of old bogey, and the future—well, that was the point of all this painful deep thinking, wasn't it? Did she have the courage to take a chance on a future that could be a wee bit better than the here and now—or far, far worse?

When Paddy O'Brien got back from Northern Ireland with the blasting caps, Maddock Lonigan made what he called "an executive decision."

"Since I'm the only one of the lot of us what's had experience with explosives, we gotta do ourselves a trial run. See how you dossers do when the bloody chips is down."

"We don't have ourselves a big supply of the dynamite," said Fergus. "We'd have to get more if we use it up."

"Not to worry, me boy. One stick is all we need. It's the *process* we have to worry on, not the result."

"We're not too flush with the blasting caps, either," said Paddy. "The bloke what sold them to me said there'd been a big call on 'em lately. He only had a few left."

"Like I said, we'll only need one."

"So where do we do this trial thing?" asked Gordie. "We don't want to get caught when we're not even doin' anything for real."

"Don't be such a puss, Gordie. Besides, who's gonna get caught? We're smarter than this whole damn bunch of Brits put together."

"So where?"

"We need to do it somewhere that won't tip 'em off to what's coming. Somewhere out in the country."

"There's not a lot of country near here," said Paddy. "We're right in the middle of one of the biggest cities in the world."

"I know a place," said Fergus. "It's out beyond where Gordie and me live. Used to ride me bike there, along a canal. It's perfect. Nothing but fields and trees and cows and the like."

"How come I don't know about this place?" said Gordie.

"Didn't want the little brother along. Needed to be by myself, to think. Had a lot to think about."

"Yeah. I guess."

"So how do we get there?" said Maddock. "You planning to ride the three of us on your handlebars?"

"Naah. I don't have me bike anyway, now. Got too big."

"So, what do we do? Fly?"

"'Course not. We take the train. Go past Northwood where we usually get off and go to the next stop. I think it's called Croxley Green, or something like that. We get off the train and it's, like, right there."

"Seems like a plan," said Maddock. "Now, let's get our supplies out here on the table and make ourselves a wee bomb. What do you say?"

Carter and Josh rode the train back from Baker Street Station to St. John's Wood in silence. Josh wanted to talk, but Carter was lost in some private place and didn't invite conversation. Josh started to make a sarcastic remark about how much studying they'd managed on the train, but Carter waved him off.

Halfway between the Tube station and school, Carter pumped a fist and shouted, "Yes."

Josh jumped and banged his hip into the corner of a red telephone booth. The lady speaking on the phone inside didn't look pleased. Josh wasn't either. "I gather you've finished your thinking," he said.

"Exactly right, my good man. Exactly. I have deduced the answer."

"Right . . . you're gonna have to fill me in on the question here."

"What the tweedy old man said. About why Arthur Conan Doyle used an address that didn't actually exist."

"So tell me, oh brilliant one, why did he?"

"Because all of his readers would want to go there. They'd stand around in front of it and stare and block the doorway and cause a huge mess. It would be awful for whoever actually lived there. Don't you see?"

"You mean, Carter, that thoughtless people would come from miles away, maybe even from places like St. John's Wood, to stare at the outside of someone's house?"

Carter waved off his friend's sarcasm and said, "You and me, you and I, are not thoughtless people. We are very thoughtful people, and we were viewing the premises with a purpose."

"You may have a thought inside that head of yours, but I don't have a clue. And what do you mean *purpose*?"

Gordie McKenna couldn't sit still. Half the time he was craning his head to study every fellow passenger boarding their train car, and half the time eying the carry-on bag sitting on the floor between Maddock's feet. His mind told him it was an innocuous piece of luggage no one could suspect of being a lethal weapon. But part of him was certain any reasonable person could sense the wires and the detonator and the slender red stick of death inside.

His older brother kept trying to distract him with inconsequential talk. Their sister's moods, their mother's health, neighborhood girls—all these things seemed to float past Gordie's head and out the window, where they got whirled away with the blur of London's suburbs. Maddock Lonigan seemed like he was oblivious to it all. He looked for all the world like he was asleep, but Gordie knew it was just an act. Maddock was a cobra with his head down, viewing his world through half-lidded eyes.

"What the devil? This ain't right." The cobra reared up and shouted at Fergus. "You said it was the next stop after yours, but this sure as hell ain't no Croxley Green."

"I thought it was," said Fergus. "Maybe it's the one after."

"Maybe you're full of it, Fergie. Maybe you're spoutin' a load a codswallop."

The next station brought an increased volume to Maddock's tirade. "Bloody hell, Fergie. It ain't this, either. This here station's called Rickmansworth, and there's no canal and no fields. Not a cow to be seen, unless you count them three old ladies sitting there stuffing their mouths full a cake."

When they saw the name Chorleywood on the next station, Maddock Lonigan cursed at the top of his lungs, grabbed the backpack, and lunged for the door. Fergus and Gordon had to scramble for their own things so they could follow their leader out onto the platform. Maddock was still cussing and waving his arms around when the train pulled out. The other passengers who'd gotten off with them made wide circles around the apparently deranged trio, escaping to the station door.

Young Gordon was calmest of the three. He stood still, thinking a minute, then said, "The map."

"Huh?"

"At every station there's a map of the whole London Underground train system. We find the map, find where we are, and how to get where we want to go."

"Good thinking, li'l bro," said Fergus. Maddock just grunted.

They found the map on the outside wall of the ticket office. Gordon traced the thin red line for the track they were on and said, "See? Here's where we went wrong. The Metropolitan Line splits, and some trains go north, some turn east. We took the wrong train. All we gotta do is go back a couple of stops and take the other branch. See, there's Croxley Green right there. Just like Fergie said."

Retracing their steps and then waiting for the right train took about an hour, during which Maddock Lonigan's temper didn't subside a bit. Fergus thought it was another example of Lonigan's unsuitability to be a team leader. They were carrying a lethal weapon, for crying out loud, and ought to be as inconspicuous as possible. Not publicly carrying on like a bull elephant with an ingrown toenail.

"About time. About bloody time," Maddock bellowed, when they began slowing for Croxley Green Station. "I'm sick of this train. Hope I never have to take one again, ever."

"Don't you have to take a train to get home tonight?" asked Gordon. Lonigan gave him a withering look. Gordon hung his head down and studied his boots. He stepped to one side and let Maddock Lonigan step off onto the platform first. Lonigan said, "Lead the way, Fergie. You been here before."

Fergus said, "It's across the street and behind those houses. We got to wind left and right through some streets to get to the canal."

"Just like playing PacMan," Gordon said, excitement back in his voice.

Lonigan muttered under his breath, "Boys. Why do I have to be saddled with boys, when here we is about to do man's work?" Aloud he said, "We ain't going to be blowin' up some bug on a computer screen. Get that through your little skulls. We're goin' to be blowing up real Englishmen. I was gonna say real *live* Englishmen, but they won't be for long."

Chapter 11

"LET ME SEE IF I UNDERSTAND THIS. You're going to become Sherlock Holmes—excuse me, a *modern-day* Sherlock Homes—for the purpose of finding a *girl*? And I'm going to put my own life on hold and become your sidekick, your Watson, so you can do what? Oh, I remember, so you can *find yourself a girl*."

Carter said, "I know when you say it that way, it seems . . ."

"I'm not sure how to say it any other way."

"I thought, I just thought, if we actually stood in front of the house where Holmes lived, we'd get excited, you'd get excited, about getting into the detective business."

"Carter, you may have deduced what the old guy meant when he left us, but let me give you another puzzle. Can you *deduce* just what the heck I'm thinking right now?"

"Well . . . you're probably still a little lukewarm on the idea." Carter turned to face his friend. "But if you were really, really, totally against it, you'd have used stronger language than, 'what the heck,' so my deduction is, you could be persuaded with proper motivation."

"Are you offering me money? Did Holmes pay Watson a gonzo salary?"

"I don't actually have any money, but . . ."

"Didn't think so."

". . . but what is it you like more than anything in the world? Within reason."

"I like to watch the Mets play at Shea Stadium. I used to like to camp in the woods up in the Poconos. Comin' here put a stop to that. I like to dream about having my own place someday, a farm maybe, where I don't have to take a train to get to school, or to work. I like . . ."

"Wait. Back up. You like to camp?"

"Yeah. Sure." Josh tilted his head and squinted at Carter.

"How about I treat you to an all-expenses-paid camping trip? To somewhere really neat?"

"Yeah, right. How are you going to pay all these expenses if you don't have any money?"

"I've got a dad who does," said Carter.

"And he's willing to bankroll you and a guy he's never met?"

"I'm pretty sure he will. You see, I've done a little detecting on *him* recently. Found out a few things."

"And these—things—are going to spring us a camping trip?"

"Oh, yeah. It's not the things that are going to do it, it's my promising not to tell my mom about the things that'll do the trick."

Madeleine (Maddie) Westfall and her friends, Beverly (Babs) Kroome and Crista Cordelia (C.C.) Piper established their watch post on the bench closest to the Rickmansworth Station office. Since there were three of them, there was no convenient place on the bench for their food and drink, but Maddie had anticipated this problem by bringing along a lovely green-and-yellow-checked picnic blanket, which she spread out in front of them on the platform floor, to accommodate their afternoon tea.

C.C. looked from the blanket to the commuters nearby and then at Maddie, raising her eyebrows.

"Pay no attention to people," said Maddie. "At our time of life, we're entitled to a few eccentricities."

"Quite so," said Babs. "Besides, we're providing a service. Entertaining the weary travelers." They did, in fact, acquire more than one puzzled look and a few rolled eyes.

"We would garner far more stares," said C.C., "if we arranged our picnic at the end of the platform and had to sprint to catch the boy."

"Absolutely," said Maddie. "Not to mention how the boy himself would feel if we attacked him like in a rugby scrum." All three women laughed at the image and slapped their knees. More than one person edged a bit further down the platform.

Three trains outbound from London disgorged passengers, who filed by the waiting friends, heading for the station door and home. The character of the throng changed gradually from shoppers, mostly women, to business types, mostly men, with each train. A few did seem to be youngsters on their way home from school, but their target wasn't among them.

"Well, he may have had a day off. Or stayed after for football practice, or anything," said C.C. "Shall we try again tomorrow?"

"One more train," said Maddie. "When I met him last time, we were on a late train. I know because of all the hooligans going to Wembley Stadium."

Sure enough, when the next train rolled in, they caught a glimpse of a young man in one of the front cars, talking animatedly with an older man sitting next to him.

"I think that's him," Maddie Westfall shouted. "It is. It is."

The three friends jumped to their feet. C.C. Piper said, "Yuck. I stepped on the lemon tortes."

"All in the line of duty, C.C. I'm sure your sneakers have been in worse."

"I'll rescue C.C.'s feet and clean up our picnic," said Babs. "You go tackle your young man, Maddie. We'll be over here, cheering you on."

Madeleine Westfall placed herself halfway between the car where she'd seen her quarry and the station exit. As the passengers started to get off the train, she composed herself and tried to look casual. She wanted the boy to think this was nothing more than a chance meeting. The truth would never do.

When she saw him step onto the platform, she knew for certain he was the one she was looking for. But something was wrong. The face she remembered as thoughtful and kind was twisted in anger. She watched as he turned abruptly away from the older man beside him and thrust away some tears with the back of a clenched hand.

As they got closer, she could hear snatches of conversation.

". . . not going to be threatened by the likes . . ."

"What about her? How do you think she'll . . ."

"Just shut up. Not your business . . ."

". . . it is my business, I'm part of this family . . ."

When they neared, the young man's eyes met hers and opened in recognition for a brief second. Then he quickly turned away from her as he walked on past. *Tears*, she thought. *The poor lad doesn't want to be seen with tears on his face.*

Babs and C.C. descended on her as soon as the departing passengers had cleared the platform.

"I guess it wasn't him," said C.C. "What a pity."

"You seemed so certain," said Babs. "Oh, well, perhaps tomorrow."

"I'm having second thoughts about this," said Maddie Westfall. "Perhaps we should just call this an interesting little excursion and give the *Cock and Crow* our business in future."

To herself, she vowed to get to the bottom of whatever troubles her young man was having. Without her friends. The man who had been berating him was certainly his father, and she knew it was surely bad form to meddle in family affairs. But the boy had looked so stricken with—with what? Fear, guilt, shame? Whatever it was didn't belong on the face of the young man who had so gallantly helped her off the train. Foolish as she knew it was to pry into a stranger's personal life, she couldn't help herself. But this was something she had to do herself, alone. Her friends would never understand. *The question is, Madeleine Westfall, do you understand it yourself?*

"I don't understand," said Fergus. "I'm sure the canal was right through there."

"These look like new houses along here," said Gordon. "Maybe they got built after you were here last."

"Could be. Can you see over any of them fences?"

"I can't see much. Maybe there are fields there."

Maddock said, "Lotta good they'll do us since they're back there and we're out here."

"Look down that street," said Gordon. "Some kinda neighborhood park or something there."

It was. And at the back end, a footpath led through a scrub of myrtles to another, wider path that ran along a narrow canal. On the far side were the fields and cows that Fergus had described, but unfortunately for their purposes, a line of narrow houseboats were tied up on the near side of the canal. Some boats seemed empty, but others had shirtless suntanned men engaged in housekeeping chores or lounging on deck with a can of beer in hand. On one boat, a young woman was lying on her stomach with her bra strap unfastened. Gordon nearly tripped over his brother, who had stopped to take in the scene.

Maddock had stopped, too, but not to admire the feminine scenery. Fergie could almost see the thoughts coursing wildly through the boss's brain. *Two hours. More than two hours on a friggin' train with two PacMan-playing imbeciles, to find a damn flotilla of idiots parked in the damn canal so we can't do what we come to do with a bit of privacy.*

Again it was Gordon who managed to find a way around the problem. "Since there's boats parked here, there's got to be one a them locks up ahead to keep the water level high along this part. There's usually a bridge across the canal at the locks."

They found the lock about a quarter-mile ahead. The water on the far side was several feet lower than the water level where they were. The lock consisted of two gates across the stream, which could be opened and closed separately. When a boatman needed to go from the lower level to the upper, he would call for the lock-keeper, who stayed in a small cottage close by. He would open the lower gate, and the boat would go into the space between the gates. Then the keeper would close the lower gate and open the other one, letting water flood in until the boat rose to the level of the higher canal. As Gordon had assumed, there was a bridge, too, and the trio of dynamiters crossed over.

It took about fifteen minutes' walk along the canal again before they found a spot away from the lock-keeper's eyes and half-naked sunbathing boaters. Fergus tried to smile and nod his head whenever they passed a lone hiker or a bicyclist, but it wasn't easy, considering their mission. They found a place where a small tree had fallen across the barbed-wire fence, letting them cross into the field with a minimum loss of blood.

"This'll do," said Lonigan. "This'll do right nice. Feel the wind out here? Feels fresh. Not like bloody London with all that smog and crap."

"Feels to me like a storm comin'," said Fergie.

"Naaa. Just wind. Don'tcha know boys. *We're* the windstorm. And these Englishers won't see us coming. Won't have a clue."

They were in the middle of a large grassy area. The trees and houses along the canal were just a smudge on the horizon, and they were just as far from humans in every other direction. They weren't far from a small group of cows, who looked up from their grazing to see who had trespassed on their territory. Apparently satisfied, they lowered their heads and went on munching.

"All right, let's do this thing," said Maddock Lonigan. "Reach in that pack and gimme the dynamite, Gordie. Fergie, you hook them two wires to the blasting cap, like we did back at the warehouse. Okay, now to the batteries and then to the timer. Don't let them wires touch, or you'll be meetin' your old dad sooner'n you wanted." He nodded his head, satisfied. "Now, you two stand back, and I'll set the timer. I'll make it just three minutes. We don't got all day."

When Fergus stood, he backed into something soft. He jumped to the side and plowed into his brother, and they went sprawling in the weeds. He looked up to see one of the brown-and-white cows giving him a quick glance to see this human thing he'd nosed into. The cow kept moving toward the target of her real interest, the little box with the round stick attached to it, being held by the other human thing. Something good to eat, probably. Why else would these humans be here? This other human didn't see her coming and wasn't prepared for the sudden appearance of a brown bovine nose pushing him aside and heading for the box of treats. As he tried to shove her aside, he twisted his body so his right foot kicked the box.

The explosion was deafening. The cow jerked sideways, stumbled, and fell. As she painfully regained her feet, she saw two of the humans holding onto their ears. Before running off to rejoin her herd, she took one look back at the third human, who wasn't holding onto anything. He was flat on his back with his arms and legs splayed out. One of his arms looked shorter than the other.

Chapter 12

*F*IONA KNEW EXACTLY WHERE TO FIND the young man she intended to bring fresh air into her life. She knew little about him, but she knew enough. He was a student at the American School in London; his name was Carter. And he had that innocent, open face she'd seen on so many Americans. And—he had risked getting that face smashed by a pack of drunken soccer hoodlums in order to rescue her.

The only problem she had in finding this Carter was escaping from her mother's constant need for attention. Not to mention the role of housemaid she'd come to play in her brothers' lives. Another trip to London was needed.

"So where ya off to, sis?"

"Someone needs to bring the food for the table, don't they?"

"So where's your shoppin' bag, then?"

"I dunna have much to buy. Not enough to burden meself with a bag."

"That's good. I'm feelin' really peckish," said Fergus. "Haven't eaten yet today. Glad ya won't be long."

"Well, I might be a tad longer than you'd like. Got to go to the greengrocers after I get me tinned goods." Fiona figured there was no sin in lying to her brother, since he'd lied to her plenty about goin' to the pub and all. "And what's to prevent you from makin' yourself a bite a somethin' anyway? Why is your stomach my business and none a your own?"

"I got more important things to do."

Fiona found she had to bite her tongue to keep from blurting out the truth—that she knew full well her two brothers were up to their necks in something truly awful. Gordie had been walking around in a daze for days. He and Fergie had gone off one morning all upbeat and looking forward to what they'd hinted was going to be an adventure in the country. They hadn't returned until after dark, and both insisted they were dead knackered and went straight to bed. Fergie had been covered in dried mud and grass stains. Gordie'd been wearing a brown shirt she'd never seen before. It looked five sizes too big and hung halfway down to his knees. The next morning Fergie shrugged off her questions, telling her to "stick to yer own business," and Gordie was a zombie. He'd been that way for three days. *Whatever happened on their "adventure," she thought, was more than my twin brother could handle.* Gordie was always the sensitive one, more so than Fergie. Not even as tough as Fiona. To see him this way felt as if a part of herself was hurting, and she didn't know why. He'd taken to shutting her out of his life, and that was the hardest thing of all.

All the more reason to find her Carter. She rubbed her eyes and shook her head. *What if he's the same? What if he's forgotten all about me, and I'm thinking like a fool? He has his own life. Maybe a girlfriend. Maybe . . .*

She saw Kerry Girl was looking up at her with those soulful eyes. *She knows, doesn't she? She knows I'm hurting and wants so bad to help.*

"Well, girl, I'm gonna have to help myself this time. I don't know if I'm going out on a fool's journey, but I have to do it. I'll tell you all about it when I get home. You be a good girl till I get back."

At the Northwood Train Station, the ticket seller asked her if it would be round-trip or one-way.

"Round-trip," said Fiona. In a faint voice, she added, "Unfortunately."

Carter was kicking himself. He just wasn't cut out to be a blackmailer. Didn't think he'd have the guts to stick with it and to hell with how it made him look. *Dad's the one that's done the dirty, not me. Why do I feel bad?* Still, once he'd gotten it in his head to do it, he had to give it a try. He'd told Josh Weaver about his plan, so he'd seem like a real wimp if he backed out now.

He'd taken the Tube into downtown London and waited outside the Knightsbridge Station where his father would board the train home. Of course, his dad just might have decided this was one of the nights when he'd skip going home and head off the other way with his perky little secretary, Miss Frampton. *Maybe I'll catch them arm-in-arm or something. Won't that be a hoot?*

As it turned out, he saw his father scurrying down the sidewalk, alone, swinging his briefcase five minutes after 6:00 p.m. His jacket was open, and his red-and-blue-striped tie was flapping in the breeze caused by his own rush. There was only a slight pause when he recognized his son, and Carter had to make a quick U-turn to keep up on the way into the station.

"What the heck are you doing here?" This was delivered over one shoulder as Carter's dad stepped onto the down-escalator. He didn't wait for a reply and wasn't even content to let the escalator do its thing, as he started to rush down step-by-step as if he were on solid stairs. Carter had to do the same thing or watch his father disappear into the bowels of the Knightsbridge Tube Station.

Some fifty feet below the streets of London, they mingled with the crowd of commuters who all seemed to be in as much of a hurry as Dad. Carter couldn't figure out why the rush. They had to stand on the platform waiting for the subway train anyway. Besides, if they missed one train, another would be along in just a few minutes. He hoped he'd never feel like joining the rat race like Dad and these other people. Then he wondered if his father had felt the same when he was young.

They rode in silence most of the way home. Dad had taken some papers out of his briefcase and made a big point of studying them. He never did get around to repeating his original question of "What the heck are you doing here?" *Thanks, Dad. You're making it a lot easier for me to do what I'm here to do.*

His chance came halfway between Pinner Station and North Harrow, when the crush of commuters had thinned and he could talk to his dad without sharing the message with a dozen strangers. Also his father had closed up his briefcase and was staring out the window. Carter decided to just flat-out ask for the camping trip money first. See where that went.

"Can't do it," said Dad. "Got too many expenses right now."

Carter swallowed hard. Suddenly his doubts were swept away. He blurted out, "You mean things like dinner and jewelry for Miss Frampton?"

The conversation went downhill from there. When they'd reached Rickmansworth, they were practically shouting at each other, heedless of other ears still close enough to hear. By the time they'd gotten off the train and were heading for the parking lot, Carter was fighting back tears and wishing he'd chickened out before he'd even started.

In the car, Dad sat behind the wheel, making no move to insert the key and start the engine. He stared out the windshield, saying nothing.

"Dad, I just . . ."

"You're just butting into things that aren't your business."

"It's *my* mother you're cheating on. How isn't it my business? I don't understand."

"Someday you will. Till then, keep your nose out of it."

Carter watched his dad clenching the steering wheel so hard the tendons in the back of his hands were showing.

"You remember when I was maybe thirteen? We went for a walk, and you gave me this talk about sex. I remember it like yesterday. I never felt closer to you than I did that day, having you tell me about all that grownup stuff. It made me feel important."

Carter's dad took his hands off the steering wheel and rubbed the back of his neck. He exhaled, closed his eyes, and gave a weak smile. After a moment, he said, "I remember it, too. Maybe it made you feel important, but it made me feel—not embarrassed exactly, but uncomfortable."

"Why?"

"I don't know. I think every father feels the same. In our world we don't talk about sex, except for dirty jokes. And then you have to have a serious conversation about it with your kid, who'd been just that, a kid, all those years."

"But I wasn't a kid anymore. That's the point."

"I know. But still . . ."

"Let me tell you a couple of things you told me in that conversation, Dad. You told me sex was such a powerful thing, you had to be really careful with it. Tried to scare me with talk about diseases and making babies I couldn't support."

"All true."

"Sure, but you took it one step further. You said sex was part of a contract between two people who loved each other. That was your word—contract. That's why it ought to be kept just for people who were married to each other. That's what you said."

Carter's dad started the car, but he didn't put it in gear. He turned and stared at his son. "So now it seems you're turning the tables and lecturing me."

"Maybe so. Tell me, how does your secretary fit into the story?"

"You really can't understand. I have needs. Your mother . . ."

"Whoa. This is stuff I really don't need to know. But look, Dad, I'm not blind. Mom's gone off into her own little world, with her bottle of vodka or whatever. But I'm not stupid, either. I figured she'd taken up drinking because she felt she'd lost you, not the other way around."

Halfway home, Carter broke the silence. "So, let me get this straight. If I were to meet a girl who really turned me on, I could just go as far with her as I wanted."

"No. That's not right."

"Seems like it."

Carter's father drove on for another block, then pulled over to the curb and stopped. "Okay, you win. Let's strike a deal here."

"A contract."

"All right, a contract."

"Go on."

"Let's take it back to that conversation we had when you were thirteen. You remember everything I said, and I'll—well, I'll try to live up to it, too."

"No more Miss Frampton?"

"Not outside of work. And one other thing—you won't tell your mom about her or any of this."

"Agreed. Now let's talk about one other thing. How about the money for that camping trip?"

The nameplate at the reception desk at ASL, the American School in London, read Tamatha Blake. Madeleine Westfall expected Ms. Blake to speak with an American accent. Instead, she spoke with the voice of a woman who had spent years trying to rid her proper British public-school voice of traces of her East-End London Cockney origins. When Maddie told her about her quest, the secretary was pleasant, but not especially helpful.

"We have a number of students who live in Rickmansworth," she said. "If you had a name . . ."

"No. I'm afraid I have no name. He has dark brown hair and is almost six feet tall. Quite slim. A good-looking young man."

The receptionist smiled and shook her head. "I'm sorry, but that could describe many boys. Besides, not many students have a need to come into the office. I'm sorry."

"Well, thank you," said Maddie. "I'll wait outside until school is out."

Out on Loudon Road, she found a low brick wall enclosing a planter of shrubbery and sat. Normally happy with her trim body, she wished she had a bit more flesh on her bones. The bricks were hard and jagged, but standing in one spot for who-knows-how-long would be worse. She watched the main door of the school and hoped the subject of her search wouldn't leave by a back way. She wondered how long she would have to wait. *Oh, well, Madeleine Westfall, what better things do you have to do with your time?*

When the dark-haired young lady stood in front of her counter, Tamatha Blake smiled and said, "May I help you, dear?"

"I hope so," said Fiona. "I'm trying to find one of your students."

"Is it an emergency?"

"Oh, no. I just need to talk to him."

The secretary looked at the clock. "We're into the last period. I'll tell you what I can do. If it's important, I'll send a note around to his classroom and ask him to meet you here after school. What's his name?"

"I don't know. I mean, only his first name. Carter. At least I think it's Carter."

The secretary shook her head. "Dearie, why don't you wait outside the door and catch your boy after school?" When the dark-haired girl had left, the secretary thought, *Lordy. Lordy. What's going on here? Two in a row. Must be something in the air.*

After his sister left the house, Fergus McKenna decided to take her advice and fix himself a bite. He found an old loaf of bread. Gone stale but still edible with a hunk of cheese and a slathering of Branston pickle. He thought to ask Gordie if he wanted some, but his brother had holed himself up in his room, so Fergie decided to let him be. *Let him starve. The kid's acting like the world ended out there in the middle of that field. What a pussie.*

It had been a pretty shocking thing. The explosion, getting thrown down into the mud, and then finding Lonigan spread-eagled in the grass with one arm blown off. *Not your everyday walk in the park.* Thinking about it, it wasn't surprising it affected Gordie worse than him. Gordie had really never witnessed violence firsthand. He, Fergus McKenna, had. With his own eyes he'd seen his father cut down by a bloody Protestant bullet. He snorted a bitter laugh. *What a hoot. Thinkin' I got an advantage 'cause I saw me old man die. Great advantage.*

It had been useful out there in the Croxley Green field, though. It let him take charge of the situation and figure out what to do. The first thing he did was make Gordie take off his shirt so he could use it as a rough tourniquet. The stump of Lonigan's arm wasn't bleeding as fierce as it might have been, but still it was pumping some every heartbeat, and he was gonna bleed out for sure if it kept on.

The next thing was to get help, and the nearest help was half a mile away. Also, he needed to make sure everybody thought he and Gordie were just wandering by, heard the explosion, and ran over to help a stranger. The question was, should he run for help or should his brother? Either way could be bad, because Gordie was in a state of shock. He might blurt out the truth, and then they'd be in dead serious trouble. Better both brothers go get help together. Nothing more could be done here anyway, except to stand and watch Maddock Lonigan die.

It was several hours later when they learned Lonigan *had* died. They were still at the Croxley police station, giving their statements about being out for a nice walk in the countryside and hearing this strange sound and all. The stupid bobbies believed every word. They'd found an old brown shirt in a storage room and gave it to Gordie to help stop the shivering he'd been doing non-stop. It was way too big, but it worked, almost.

The coppers offered to drive them home, but Fergus insisted they take the train. He told them they needed time to clear their heads of the terrible experience. The truth was, there was no way he was going to let Mum and Fiona know anything about this matter—anything.

Tamatha Blake was straightening up her desk, preparing to go home. She'd been a receptionist at ASL for almost three years, and this was beginning to feel like a second home. Still, when the last of the rowdy students had streamed out the door, the silence in the hallways could feel a bit spooky. Her friend Amanda Peers came out of the office door, her purse slung over her shoulder. "So, how were things out here on the firing line today?"

"Same old, same old," said Tamatha. "How were things back in the caves?"

"That's where all the fun is, don't you know. Back there out of sight."

"Right. Spare me."

As they were heading out the door, Tamatha told her friend about the two strange requests she'd just had. Two different people asking to see students whose names they didn't know. "Do they think I'm some kind of psychic? Able to guess which kid they mean, out of hundreds and hundreds?"

As they neared the Tube station, Tamatha whispered in her friend's ear. "You know those two people I told you about? We just passed them. The old lady's still sitting there on the planter, waiting. We should have told her the kid's are all gone, so she can quit her waiting."

"She'll figure it out soon enough."

"The other one's that girl we just passed, sauntering along, looking back over her shoulder every two seconds, like the kid she's wanting is gonna bust out the door behind her. At least she knew more about her boy than the old lady did about hers. Knew his first name was Carter."

Amanda stopped and grabbed her friend's arm. "Carter. That's strange. A man came in earlier wanting to collect his son, Carter Chamberlain."

"I didn't see him."

"Probably you were on your break. Anyway, he said he needed to get the boy because it was some sort of family emergency. I sent for him, and the two of them left."

"I sure wish I'd known . . ."

"I don't think it was much of an emergency, though. At first the boy didn't seem too happy to see his father, but then they stopped at the door and talked. Couldn't hear what was said, but the boy finally pumped his fist like he'd won the pools or something. Then the father put his arm around him, and they went out the door laughing. Some emergency."

Josh Weaver was frustrated. He'd lain awake half the night thinking about his new friend Carter's weird idea to team up and do detective work. He'd finally made up his mind and was planning to tell Carter about it after school. Then, in Chemistry, a girl from the office brought a note in for the teacher. Mr. Franks called Carter up front and whispered something in his ear. Carter didn't look happy, but he stomped out the door after the girl who brought the note.

After last period, Josh rushed to intercept Carter between the Social Studies classroom and the lockers, so he could give him his decision. He'd been rehearsing it in his mind. *Don't think I've decided it isn't a stupid idea, but I've made up my mind to give it a try. Just for you. I might need a favor someday, so you'll owe me. Got it? You'll owe me.* When the last student straggled out of the Social Studies classroom, Josh stuck his head in the door. No Carter. The teacher held up her hands, palm up, and said Carter had missed class. "If you see him tonight, tell him we're having a test on Chapter 23."

"Uh. Right. I don't usually see him after school but . . ."

"Well, if you do."

"Chapter 23."

On his way home, Josh thought about his new friend Carter, whose mind seemed to be churning out weird things all the time. In the Weaver family, Josh's sister was the wild one. She was always thinking of ways to get herself in trouble and ways to talk herself out of the mess. Josh was the cautious one, never taking a chance if he wasn't sure of the outcome, never playing a sport or a game he wasn't absolutely sure of winning. He thought it more than a little strange that the first thing he needed to do, now that he'd plucked up the courage to be a world-class detective, was to figure out how to get hold of his leader, but he didn't have a clue how to do it. *Good going, Watson. Sherlock will be so proud.*

Outside the American School, Fiona waited until the stream of students had trickled away to nothing. *Wouldn't you know it, I come all this way, tell a few fibs to me brother, and my Carter doesn't show.* She decided to wait just a few more minutes. The pavement in front of the school doors was now totally empty. The last of the students could be seen rounding the corner to the Tube station or being picked up in cars by waiting parents. The only person still around was an old woman, sitting uncomfortably on a brick planter, and anxiously watching the door. *Good luck, old lady. Hope you find whoever you're waiting for. I'm sure not finding mine.* When Fiona finally gave up and started a slow walk back to the train, the old lady hadn't moved. *I don't guess she's got hungry, nasty-tempered brothers waiting at home.*

When a young woman from the school office brought a note to Mr. Franks in Chemistry, Carter hadn't paid much attention until he saw the teacher look his way. When he crooked a finger with a come-here gesture, Carter looked over his shoulders to see if someone else was being summoned. Probably not. When he tapped on his chest, Mr. Franks nodded and gave him a tilted-head grin that said, "Who else would it be, moron?"

The note said to come to the office because Carter's father was waiting. *Oh, oh. Must be trouble. Maybe Mom finally drank too much, fell, and hit her head. Maybe something happened to Amy. Maybe Gwen called from Colorado with some bad news.*

When he got to the office, his father looked serious, but he wasn't pacing or sweating or anything like that. He wouldn't tell Carter what had happened.

"Outside. Tell you outside."

That frightened Carter even more. Apparently it was something so serious, Dad didn't want the office staff to hear about it.

At the door, Carter stopped and said, "Okay. We're alone now. Tell me what it is. You got me really scared."

"It's nothing really. Just thought the two of us should spend some time together is all. Haven't done much of that for a while."

Carter shook his head. "What?"

"Some time to get to know each other better. You know—father and son."

"This is like some father and son *bonding* thing?"

"Well, sure. You're a man now, practically, so we can talk about things."

"Like man-to-man."

"Right."

"You know the school year's almost over. Final exams next week. And I've got all kinds of cramming to do to get up to speed."

"You can handle it. You always have. Besides, I've been thinking about this camping trip thing, and I'm ready to stake you a good one. First class."

Carter pumped his fist. *Yeah!* Dad draped his arm over Carter's shoulder, and they went out the door, laughing. "Remember the time we got caught in the rain? Nearly washed our tent away."

"You'd think a great camper like yourself would know to dig a ditch around the tent."

"It was summer."

"It was Texas."

They stopped at a small deli run by a thin-faced Pakistani man and bought some salami, bread, and cheese. "A jug of wine would go well with this, don't you think?" said Carter. "You know—'a Jug of Wine, a loaf of bread—and thou beside me singing in the wilderness'."

"Right. I said you were *almost* a man, not actually one. Showing off and quoting Omar Khayyam won't do you any good."

"Hey, just testing. No harm in that."

They went south and east until they came to Regent's Park. After they'd walked along some footpaths and across a wide expanse of lawn, they found a picnic table with benches and spread out their meal. Carter looked around and decided Regent's Park was the biggest he'd ever seen.

"You know, Dad, Sherlock Holmes was supposed to have lived just on the edge of this park."

Carter's dad's mouth was full of bread and salami, so he just grunted. The grunt was enough, though, to tell Carter his dad didn't give a flip about where Sherlock Holmes had lived. Carter decided the whole detective business was something he'd keep to himself anyway. He really was by himself. His new buddy Josh Weaver had sure let him know how *he* felt about it. Well, maybe the promised camping trip would change his mind. Maybe.

"So you're going to help me and Josh go camping soon as school's out?"

"Sure am."

"First class."

"Absolutely. Nothing too good for my boy. I'm thinking of the Lake Country up in Northern England, or maybe even the Scottish Highlands. How does that sound?"

Carter felt he was in some kind of fantasy movie. The wizard comes around in the night and touches his dad with a magic wand and, *presto,* new dad appears. Then the truth came to him in a flash. He thought of that old movie where Marlon Brando talks like he has marbles in his mouth. Brando was the Godfather who was the head of this Mafia crime family. He'd do something for people when they were in trouble and then tell them he'd collect his debt someday when *he* needed a favor. Usually it was years later, and usually it was something bad they didn't want to do, but they had no choice. He'd made them an offer they couldn't refuse.

Now, Carter thought, *I'm the Godfather. Dad owes me big time for keeping my mouth shut, and this camping trip—it's an offer he can't refuse. Wizard!*

Chapter 13

GORDON MCKENNA KNEW HIS BROTHER thought he was being childish, but he couldn't help himself. Struggling to regain his footing after the blast, seeing Maddock Lonigan there on the ground with blood pouring out of his stump of an arm, parts of the arm itself glistening in the grass, it felt like the ground was opening up, trying to swallow him. He'd sunk back to his knees, unable to move even though Fergie was buzzing around like mad. He'd barely shrugged when his shirt was stripped over his head. He didn't react at all to the sight of its light blue color slowly disappearing in a flood of bright red. It felt like watching a movie, a violent, scary movie, but he knew in the back of his mind he'd be walking out of the theater into the sunshine when it was over.

But, it never was over. When they ran to the canal lock-keeper's home for help, he was always a step behind Fergie, even though he was the faster runner. He was quite happy to stand back and let his brother do all the talking. When someone came with the news that Lonigan had died, it seemed like just a continuation of the movie. No reason to feel anything.

He was feeling things now. For three days, Fiona had refused to let him starve and forced him to eat at least some of the food she brought to his room. He was beginning to come out of his dream-state, and he could feel a restless energy running through him. It should have felt good, but it didn't. It was worse, much worse, to replay in his mind the horror of what his brother was calling "that thing in the field."

The worst thing, though, was the fact he couldn't reconcile his reaction to seeing Lonigan killed with what they'd been working for months to do—blow up people. Yeah, he knew it was all for a good cause, to make the British get out of Ireland for good. He'd been raised knowing all about the way Protestant Britain had invaded and mistreated Catholic Ireland for hundreds and hundreds of years. How even now, their iron-fisted rule in Northern Ireland was like a cancer. They'd killed his father!

Still, he, Maddock Lonigan, Paddy O'Brien, and Fergie were going to kill people here in London. Sure they'd planned to target soldiers and policemen, but some innocent people were sure to be killed, too. Besides, he'd seen what a bomb could do. They never showed the bloody bits of flesh in the movies.

Fergie didn't even bother to knock when he came barging in.

"Get yer butt outta that bed and show some life, ya bloody ponce. Time to quit yer moping and do something. I got in mind beatin' the pants offen ya in a game a darts."

He grabbed some trousers off the chair and threw them at Gordie. "Here. You're gonna need a pair a pants on if I'm gonna beat 'em off."

Outside, Gordie blinked in the sunlight. It had been a while since he'd seen more than a few rays leaking through the slats of his bedroom blinds. He studied the street he'd known for almost half his life, trying to get his mind out of that Croxley Green field. He noticed things he'd never paid any attention to before. The builders of the brick row-houses across the street had tried to give their creations some undeserved class by putting stone archways over the doorways. They'd even added a few carved gargoyles here and there to give the place the feel of some old cathedral or something. Gordie thought it probably hadn't worked, even when it was new. Now it was just pitiful, with the brick, the stone, and the gargoyles all stained black from hundreds of years of rain and coal fires.

Down at the corner, a small shop had faded gold letters that read, "Papers, Mags, Cigs." And Mrs. Roberts, right next door, spent hours in the tiny square of dirt in front of her house, tending a profusion of flowers in every possible color. Dead flowers were picked the second they started to wilt. Heaven help a caterpillar that happened to wander into Mrs. Roberts' turf. The McKenna front garden couldn't be any different. There were two or three weeds struggling in hard-packed brown earth. Kind of like the people *inside* the house. Every bloody one of them living just half a life, hanging on to what might have been and probably never will be.

Gordie's somber thoughts were interrupted by a gruff voice. "You're the McKennas. Right?" A man wearing a dark blue windbreaker and a checked cloth cap stood a few feet away. He held his chin with one hand. The other was stuffed casually in his trouser pocket.

"Who wants to know?" said Fergus.

"If you're not the McKenna boys, you got no reason to know. If you are, I'll tell ye."

Fergus looked over at Gordon and squinted his eyes. Gordie shrugged.

"We might be they," said Fergie. "And depending on who you be, might not. Your call."

The man snorted and laughed, although Gordie could tell he wasn't really amused. "All right. I'm Sean Haverty, a fella you're goin' to get to know very well. If, of course, you're the McKenna lads. It'll be easy enough to find out, when I knock on that door you just come out."

"No you don't," said Fergie. "You don't need to be knockin' on that or any other door hereabouts. We're they."

"Of course, I knew that. Knew the minute I seen ye. Paddy O'Brien described ye perfect."

Gordon felt a sudden hollow place in his gut. He was just thinking Lonigan's death, terrible as it was, had a bright side. He and Fergie could go about the business of living, with their deadly project buried in the past. Now here was someone who was bringing it all back. He spoke up, for almost the first time in three days. "What—what is it you're wanting, Mister? . . ."

"Haverty. But of course you'll be calling me Sean. We like to keep it simple in the movement. It's easier, and safer."

"So you're, like, taking over from Lonigan?" asked Gordie.

"You got it. We were plannin' on replacing him even before he was stupid enough to get hisself killed."

Fergie pumped his fist. "Yes. Been thinking all along he wasn't cut out to be a leader. I coulda done a better job meself."

"Well, no need for that now. I'm here," said Haverty. "And we got work to do. Got less than two weeks to bring things all together. Boys, we got a timetable, and I'm here to see it gets kept."

The empty spot in Gordie's stomach had become a knot that hurt so bad he could barely keep from doubling over. "I'm not gonna do it. Fergie, tell him. I'm just not cut out for this stuff. I'd just get in your way. I can't do it. I can't."

Before Fergus could say anything, Haverty interrupted. "That's not acceptable. Fergus, your job will include keeping your little brother in line. If he can't manage to do anything useful, we have to at least make sure his hands are as dirty as the rest of us. If he gets it in his mind to tell the bloody British coppers about what we're doin', I want to make sure he's the first to end up behind bars. I'm already of a mind to tell them coppers up in Croxley Green that our Gordie, here, was the one what set off the bomb that killed poor innocent Mr. Lonigan."

"But that's just . . ."

"Just a taste of what you're in for if you don't keep to the plan. Did you think you could just waltz away?"

"Well, sure. Why not?"

"Let me tell you something, laddie. This ain't no kid's game we're playing. This is big time, and we got one rule that nobody, I mean nobody, can break."

Gordie didn't say anything. He stood quietly staring with glazed eyes at Sean Haverty, knowing full well what words would come next.

"In the movement, no one quits. No matter what, nobody quits. *Nobody.*"

Chapter 14

MADELEINE WESTFALL DECIDED SHE'D better revert back to Plan A, since Plan B had cost her half a day and come up empty. The platform of the Rickmansworth Station was close to home, after all, and she knew the boy would come through there eventually. *Next time,* she thought, *he'll be alone. And he won't be crying.* The sight of that tearful face was painful to remember. And the anger pouring out of the father's eyes, that was dreadful, too.

What will the boy think when he sees me? She knew he had recognized her that terrible day and had turned away embarrassed. Would he still be self-conscious about it? She decided her best approach would be to pretend it never happened. If he brought the subject up, she'd respond the best she could, but unless he did, she would act like this was their first meeting since that first time on the train.

The very next day, she took up her position on the station bench. It was the same bench she and Babs and C.C. had sat on to enjoy their picnic. This time she was all alone, until a young girl walked in from the ticket office doorway. The girl looked around nervously, then decided on the very bench where Maddie sat. Maddie smiled and moved over to give the girl more space.

The dark-haired young girl glanced sideways at her benchmate, clearly trying to make up her mind about something. Finally, she said, in a timid voice, "Ma'am, I think I saw you yesterday. In London." She shook her head. "I'm sorry, that's daft, it musta been someone looks like you. I'm sorry." She turned away and stared at the double ribbon of steel disappearing into the distance.

"I was in London yesterday, child. But I can't imagine you would take notice of an old woman like me."

"Not so old. No older than me mum, anyway."

"I was in St. John's Wood," said Madeleine, "on a quest that turned out to be in vain."

The girl had turned completely toward Madeleine and was staring with her mouth open. Finally, she stuttered, "You, you were s-sitting on the planter outside the school. I remember now. You looked lost."

"Oh, I wasn't lost, my dear. I knew exactly where I was. The young man I was looking for was the one who couldn't be found."

"I couldn't find mine, either. I waited for hours."

"You were waiting for a young man, too?"

"Yes, I know it's silly. I only met him once. On the train coming out of London. I'll never forget what he did on that train. Did for me."

Madeleine's mind was spinning. Spinning back in time to the day when her chivalrous young man had helped her off the train. Back to the hellish ride it had been as far as Wembley Park where the soccer hooligans made their welcome exit.

"He kept you from being molested by those ruffians, didn't he?"

The girl blinked. "How did you know?"

"I was there. Huddled in my seat with my meager purchases, hoping those drunken louts would leave me alone. That same young man who helped you, helped an old lady, too. Helped her remember there were decent young people in the world."

"So, the person, the person you're looking for is . . ."

"I think you are probably correct, child. I think you and I are looking for the very same young man."

"Blimey," said the dark-haired young girl.

"Well said," added the silver-haired Madeleine Westfall.

Earlier that day, Josh Weaver had met Carter in the hallway between first and second periods. "I looked for you after school. I wanted to tell you I'd decided to help with your crazy detecting business. Just for the fun of it. Not because I think you really need to find this mysterious girl."

"Cool."

"Where the heck were you yesterday?"

"My dad came and took me outta school. Can you believe? Told the school it was a family emergency."

"And it wasn't?"

"Not in the usual sense. Dad did think he had a crisis to solve with his son."

"That son being . . ."

"You got it. Me. I got up the courage to do what we talked about. The thing with his secretary. He freaked."

"I don't doubt it. So what happened?"

"We yelled and screamed at each other. Whataya think? But then he caved, and I kinda took over. Like I was in charge."

"Get outta here."

"No. I mean it. I was in total control. He was groveling at my feet."

"You're shittin' me."

"Well, a little bit. He didn't actually grovel, but he did say he was sorry for what he did, cheating on my mother and all."

"More likely sorry for getting caught."

"I thought of that, but hey, I'll take it any way it comes. Worked out the same for me. And you."

"So the camping trip is on?"

"First class. The minute this school nonsense is over, we're outta here. What do you think about Scotland? Loch Ness. All that."

"Wow. How do we get there?"

"By car. Dad's gonna drive."

"Your dad is going with us?"

"Yeah. Forgot to mention that little detail. But not to worry. He'll be on his best behavior. After all, he's the one that's dancing, and I'm the one holding the strings."

Fiona was still amazed this old lady sitting next to her on the bench had been looking for the same bloke she was. The woman said she had an even tougher time with the school receptionist because she didn't even know Carter's first name. *Lot of good it did me, knowing his name was Carter. I still ended up with bugger all.*

"I'm looking for Carter because he was kind to me, and I just want to get to know someone who has restored my faith in the younger generation," said the woman. "I suspect you have something quite different in mind."

"What do you mean?"

"Don't be coy, girl. Romance is what I mean."

"No, no. It's different than that. Deeper than that, actually." Fiona gave a tight smile and shook her head. "I know you don't believe me."

"I'm a good listener."

"It's just my life is a total mess. A wreck. And I've got no one to help me get through. I thought Carter—he seems like just the sort who might . . ."

"Might give you a shoulder to cry on?"

"I guess so."

"But don't you have family? You're Irish, right? I know how important family is to the Irish."

"No family I can count on. Dad was ki . . . Dad died. When I was young. Me mum's lost her marbles. All a them."

"No brothers or sisters?"

"Two brothers, but they're part a me problem."

"At least in a couple of years you'll be away from it all. Out on your own."

"Not a chance. Someone's gotta take care of me mum. And I'm the only one who can—or will." Fiona sniffed. "I had such plans, growing up. I was goin' to get into veterinary medicine. I really love horses and wanted to spend me life taking care of them. But then . . . then I had to drop outta school. Never even got to A-levels."

"And you think this Carter can help?"

"I don't know. Oh, God. It's probably wrong what I'm wanting. Wrong to burden someone I hardly know. I really oughta go home." She started to get up.

The old lady put out her hand and stopped her. "Don't go. Let's wait for our young man together. If you leave now, you're judging him harshly. You're assuming he would feel uncomfortable helping you cope with your problems. Is that fair?"

Fiona settled back on the bench. She sighed deeply, then hesitantly extended a hand. "I'm Fiona McKenna."

"And I am Madeleine Westfall. My friends call me Maddie. I hope you'll do me the same honor."

"All right."

"I'm so glad we got that straightened out. Just in time."

"Pardon?"

"Train's coming."

Sean Haverty was everything Maddock Lonigan had not been. He was cautious, efficient, and single-minded. He was also ruthless. The idea of blowing up innocent people didn't bother him in the least. In fact, he told the McKenna boys that killing innocent people was an essential part of the plan. "The more the better, don'tcha see? The bloody British gotta know there ain't no way they can win this war, so they best tuck their tails between their legs and clear outta Northern Ireland."

He explained he was the leader of three separate groups. He called them "cells." Fergus, Gordon, and Paddy O'Brien were in Cell B.

"When do we get to meet the guys in Cells A and C?" asked Fergie.

"You don't. It's safer that way. If one of you is stupid enough to get caught, you can't finger the others, 'cause you don't know who they are."

"We'd never talk."

"When they start to pull your fingernails out, you will. Count on it."

"We do know who *you* are," blurted out Gordie. "Aren't you afraid of that?"

"You think you know who I am. But you don't know where I live. And as to me name—how can you be sure it really is Sean Haverty?"

"It's not?"

"I could call meself Mickey Mouse, and you'd be as close to the truth."

In addition to keeping the identities of the other cell members hidden, "Sean Haverty" wouldn't give them any hint as to what their targets would be. "If the coppers are there waiting for them when they do their work, won't matter *who* they are. They still get nabbed, and our work don't get done."

"When do we learn about *our* target?" said Fergie. "Seems maybe that would be a help."

Haverty thought for a moment, then said, "Guess it can't hurt now. You'll need to check it out in advance anyways. Get the lay of the land."

The brothers were instructed to go to Piccadilly Circus that evening at 7:00 p.m. Haverty and Paddy O'Brien would meet them there, and they would plan the operation in detail. "Don't be late. I don't wanta be standing there with me hands in me pockets."

In fact, they were early. Fergie thought it would be a good idea to look like they were the serious ones. Maybe O'Brien would show late and make the McKenna boys look good. At Haverty's insistence, they were wearing their finest clothes. "Wear what you'd wear to church," he'd said. When Fergie said they hadn't set foot in a church since their pa died, they were told to "wear whatever the hell you think you'd wear if you was to go to church. Geez!"

O'Brien wasn't late either. He and Haverty came up the steps from the Underground train station together, and the four of them walked the circumference of Piccadilly Circus. Gordie knew the intersection of streets had the strange name of Circus because it was a circular roundabout with an open space for people to get together and stare at the stores all around with their bright neon advertising. In the middle, there was a fountain with a massive pedestal holding a tiny bronze statue.

"Look at that thing," said Fergie. "Leave it to the stupid English to have a statue of a naked kid with wings, standing on one tiptoe and shooting a bow and arrow. Weird."

"That's supposed to be Eros, the Angel of Christian Charity," said Haverty. "Besides, he's not totally naked. He's got that sash draped across his private parts."

"It's still bloody stupid."

Gordie couldn't keep quiet any longer. "I don't understand. In school we learned something about the old Greek gods. Eros was supposed to be the god of love. Sex actually. The boys all laughed and made jokes about it. How can he be the Angel of Christian Charity?"

"Another good reason to blow these idiot Limey's all to hell," said Haverty. "They can't get nothin' right." He had to whisper this last because they found themselves in a crush of people, jostling about. Some of them were taking pictures of Eros, others of the neon signs on the buildings surrounding the Circus, advertising Coke and McDonald's and Sanyo and dozens of the world's biggest companies. Others seemed to be taking pictures of the other people.

Haverty motioned for Cell B to follow him across the street to a place where it was relatively quiet. Gordie could see his brother was bursting with excitement. "This place is perfect," said Fergie. "Even that little one-stick thing that took out Maddock in the field would sure make a splash here. Look at all these tossers crowded together. It's bleedin' deadly."

Gordie felt like curling up and disappearing down one of the cracks in the pavement. His brother had taken Haverty's lethal outlook and made it his own. Even the sight of Maddock's blood hadn't given him second thoughts. If anything, it had made him more bloodthirsty. Gordie glanced at Paddy O'Brien to see how he was taking this turn of events. If anything, Paddy's eyes were shining more brightly than Fergie's at the thought of blowing up all these innocent people.

"Actually," said Haverty, "it's not perfect. Look at all those blokes pushing and shoving out there around the statue. Listen to them talking. Hear any of 'em that ain't talkin' English?"

All three of his companions nodded. "Lots of 'em," said O'Brien.

"And the ones that are talkin' in English. Any of 'em sound American?"

"Yeah. Quite a few."

"Then maybe you can see this ain't the perfect target. It's the bloody Brits we need to clear outta Northern Ireland, not the Eye-talians or the French or the Russians or the Pakistanis. And for sure, not the Americans."

"So why did? . . ."

"Come on, this way. I got the perfect place to put on our show. Not so many people as here, but they'll be the *right* people."

Haverty led the way along Piccadilly Road until they came to an open doorway, over which a sign read "Burlington Arcade."

Over the sign were two large carved spirals that looked like rams' horns butting into each other. They were flanked by statues Gordy thought looked like grownup angels with little babies. What they call cherubs, probably.

"This is the place, lads. This is where you'll make history and make your people proud. And when we get inside there, you'll see why I told ya to wear your Sunday best."

Sure enough, when they stepped into the Arcade, Gordie stopped dead and held his breath. He stared open-mouthed at the sight of a long corridor lined with some of the fanciest, most expensive-looking shops he'd ever seen. Or imagined. The corridor was roofed over with a glass ceiling from which chandeliers hung at intervals. They made the gold and silver and jewelry in the shop windows sparkle, as if they were giving off their own light. "Cor," he said, when his breathing had resumed.

"Jaysus. Have a squizz at this place," said Fergie.

"Take a look at the people in here," said Haverty. "This is where the posh Brits and the high muck-a-mucks come to shop. These is the people whose attention we aim to get."

"I see some people that look like tourists," said O'Brien.

"Yeah, but not like out there in Piccadilly Circus. Besides, serves 'em right for comin' in here and hobnobbin' with the British toffs."

"Speakin' of toffs," said Fergie, "what kinda holy show is that comin' toward us? Looks like someone I see'd on the cover of *Oliver Twist* or another one a them old-time books."

"Aah," said Haverty. "That's one of the Beadles."

"Bull," said Fergie. "He's way too old to be one of the Beatles. Even Ringo looks better than this guy."

"Not Beatles, Beadles with a D. He's a cop, really."

"You're joking."

"Nope. It's true. When he gets near, let's see what he has to say."

"Are you crazy? We gotta turn around and get outta here—now."

"Don't be such a pussy, Fergus. We're just innocent tourists here to see the sights. Only natural we'd want to talk to him. Besides, this is the reason you're wearin' the fancy clothes."

When the Beadle neared, he touched the brim of his gold-braided top hat, bowed slightly, and said, "Good evening to you, young gentlemen."

"Good evening to you," said Haverty, in a voice that sounded to Gordie almost as much British at it did Irish. *That's a talent I'd have never expected.* Gordie's throat was still so constricted with fear, he figured he personally couldn't croak out a word in any accent.

Haverty seemed to be enjoying himself, however. "You might tell my young charges here something about yourself and what you do."

The man in the long frock-coat and top hat drew himself up and held up one finger. Gordie thought he looked like he'd been asked to address the Queen.

"I, sir, am one of the Beadles." Haverty smiled at Fergie. "I and my predecessors have been protecting this establishment since it was first built by Lord Cavendish in 1819. One hundred and sixty-three years of service."

"Very impressive," said Haverty. "Does it need much protecting?"

"Very little, thankfully. Lord Cavendish specified certain rules that we are bound to enforce, even to this day. There is to be no whistling, singing, playing of musical instruments, running, or carrying an open umbrella."

Fergie let out a short laugh, and Haverty elbowed him. "Very admirable," said Haverty in his best upper-class voice. "But surely there have been more serious matters calling for your attention in all these years."

"Well, yes. During the Second World War, the Piccadilly end was destroyed by German bombs and had to be rebuilt, but of course they were required to adhere to the original architecture."

"Of course."

"And in 1964, there was a truly horrific robbery when a Jaguar Mark 10 charged right through here at high speed. It was the first and only four-wheel vehicle to enter these hallowed premises."

"Simply awful. And what happened?"

"Six masked men armed with axe handles and iron bars smashed the windows of the Goldsmith's shop and stole jewelry worth thirty-five thousand pounds. They escaped by reversing down the length of the Arcade. After that the bollards at the entrance were introduced."

Fergie said, "Bollards. Are those the big fat posts out front that're round on top and look like giant? . . ."

Haverty gave Fergie another elbow to cut him off. "I'm sure the perpetrators of that insidious crime were soundly punished."

"'Fraid not. They were never caught."

"Pity."

"Yes. I was quite fresh at the time, and it was an appalling introduction to my new posting. I felt just terrible, terrible."

"Well, that's all in the past," said Haverty. "It's most unlikely you will ever have to suffer through an experience like that again."

"Quite so," said the Beadle. "Quite so."

"Well, I must be on my way with the young lads. I'm sure they could use some sustenance about now. It's been ages since afternoon tea."

The four of them started back for the doorway. Gordie and the others turned to watch the Beadle's backside as he retreated down the long corridor, touching his hat and bowing to each person he passed. Fergie and Paddy broke out laughing as they walked out the door. Fergie turned to Gordie and said, "Don't get excited, little brother, and play with the bollards on the way out."

During Chemistry class, Carter took Josh aside and said, "Got some news, bro. Looks like I won't be doin' any detecting after all."

"Tell me you're joking."

"Nope."

"After all that business on Baker Street and blackmailing your dad and getting me excited about a camping trip?"

"Thing is, I found Fiona. Actually, she found me. Funniest thing."

"I'm not in much of a funny mood right now, Sherlock."

"I'd think you'd be happy for me, not pissed."

"Yeh, yeh. I'm overwhelmed with joy. So, tell me, how is it this Fiona found you instead of the other way around?"

"This is where it gets weird. I get off the train yesterday afternoon, and who's waiting on the platform for me?"

"Fiona, I guess."

"No. It's this old lady I met on the train the same day I met Fiona. Her name's Madeleine, but she wants me to call her Maddie."

"So suddenly you're real tight with this old lady."

"No. Yes. Heck, I don't know. Anyway, she acts like she just happens to be standing on the platform when I get off the train, and looks surprised and all to see me, but I know she was givin' me a line. She was there to find me on purpose."

"How can you tell?"

"Well, she'd been there when I got off the train a couple of days ago, but I was in the middle of that argument with Dad, and she turned away like she was embarrassed to see it. But that's not the real reason. After she'd said all these things about how happy she was to see me, pleased as pudding actually, then she says she has a surprise for me. She motions down the platform and there she is—Fiona, standing with her hands under her chin and looking shy."

"Sheesh, Carter, forget the detecting business, you got supernatural powers. Wish for something, and presto, there it is."

"I think it's more likely she came looking for me because of incredible animal magnetism. Girls just can't get enough of me."

"Funny, I hadn't noticed a single girl paying you attention at school."

"That's because I've had my 'I'm taken' force shield up."

"Yeah, right. Spare me. So what did you and Fee-ona do then?"

"Not much. We went to this pub in Rickmansworth, the *Cock and Crow,* where Madeleine, Maddie, seems to be a regular. The place has a real old bar and another part that's more for families. That's where we went. The two females talked about how they'd met by accident, trying to find me. That's the really weird part."

"Weird that as many as two females would *want* to find you, but go on."

"Maddie said she'd been impressed with what a gentleman I'd been when I helped her off the train. She wants to introduce me to her girlfriends. Fiona wouldn't tell me why she wanted to meet me. Said she'd tell me if we could get together this afternoon."

"Sweet. So it's a real date, huh?"

"Not sure. That day on the train I'd asked if I could see her again, and she kind of blew me off. Seemed like she didn't want to, but *had* to. Now, she does want to see me, but she seems even more nervous about something. Like I said, weird."

"Carter, my man—I think everything about you is weird."

Chapter 15

CARTER KNEW SOMETHING WAS WRONG the minute he walked in the door. Even though it was getting dark, there were no lights on anywhere. He thought no one was home until he heard muffled sounds from the back part of the house. He found Amy in a hallway, curled up on the floor and crying in a way he hadn't seen in years. He thought of lifting her up, but changed his mind and sat down next to her.

He put his arm around Amy's shoulders and said, "Tell me about it, Kitten. What's the matter?"

Amy shook her head and looked away. He decided to take another approach. "Hey, Kitten, I met a couple of interesting people today. People I think you'd like a lot." Still no reaction. "One's a nice lady whose name is Madeleine. Remember that old book you used to have with a girl in it named Madeleine?"

Carter thought he could see Amy's head nod, just a little, so he kept on. "Anyway, this Madeleine isn't a young girl, she's an old lady, but she's really, really nice. If you want, I'll introduce her to you sometime. Won't that be good?"

This time there wasn't even a hint of a nod, but Carter plunged on. "The other person I met is a girl about my age. Her name's Fiona. Isn't that a pretty name? Anyway, I'm going to see her tomorrow, after school. Maybe I can bring her to meet you. If I get her here in time, I'll bring her to the bus stop."

Amy didn't nod. In fact, she shook her head wildly and started crying louder. "I'm not going. I'm not going to school tomorrow."

"Amy . . ."

"I'm never going to go to school again. I'll lock myself in my room, and you can forget about me."

Carter grabbed his sister's shoulders and spun her around to face him. "What the heck are you talking about? You crazy? You're my Kitten. I'd as soon forget about breathing than forget about you."

"Carter, I . . ."

"Now tell me, what's this about? What's going on?"

Between sobs, Amy said, "It . . . it's Mom. She yelled at me and threw a bottle at me."

"A bottle?"

"Uh, huh. It was empty, but it hit me on the leg and it hurt."

"Damn."

"She went back in her room, and I could hear her making real loud noises, like she was still throwing things and kicking stuff. A few minutes ago she got real quiet. I'm scared."

"Don't be scared, Kitten."

"I'm sorry, Carter. I didn't mean to get her mad. I was just hungry and asked if she'd . . ."

"Stay here. No, you go in the kitchen. There's a bag of crisps in the pantry. You get them out and eat all you want. Get an orange soda or something out of the fridge to wash 'em down. Save some for me when I get back. You got that?"

Amy nodded and sniffed.

"All right. Now go. Oh, and bring one of your books to read while you eat. I don't want you sitting there thinking about Mom or me or what I'm doing or anything but those crisps and that soda."

Carter wasn't sure *what* he'd be doing. The only thing he knew was *something* had to be done. It was bad enough Mom was so unhappy she'd come to drink herself stupid to escape, but now Amy. *Whatever it takes. I'll do whatever it takes to protect my Kitten.* He gave his mother's door a quick sharp knock, didn't wait for an answer, and barged into her bedroom.

She was sprawled on the bed, a leg draped off the side so one shrimp-colored slipper grazed the floor. The other slipper was halfway across the room. She was half-wearing an old light-blue terrycloth bathrobe that had slipped up to reveal more of her leg and thigh than Carter wanted to see. He jerked the bathrobe down to cover her as best he could, and lifted her drooping leg onto the bed. He struggled to pull her toward the headboard and stuffed a pillow under her head. Even though she was now passed out completely, her hair was still wet and her forehead glistened with sweat from her previous exertions.

Carter stood silently, watched her chest rise and fall, and listened to her labored breathing. He went to his parents' bathroom, dampened a cloth, and brought it back to wash his mother's face. She groaned a little, then got quiet again. When he laid the washcloth on the night stand, he saw the ugly rings her booze had left on the wood surface. Here was absolute proof the mother he remembered, the one who always insisted on coasters and place mats, was gone. This woman passed out on the bed was another person altogether.

Little by little his anger was tempered by something like embarrassment. And even a flash of sorrow for this woman in front of him. He knew if she were only halfway sober she'd be mortified with shame at displaying herself like this to her son.

So now I have a new mission in life. And I'm the only one to do it. Gwen's gone; Amy's too young. And Dad—he refuses to admit he may be responsible for her being like this. So it's just me. Somehow, some way, I've got to get our mom back.

When Fiona got to Northwood station, she took a seat to wait for the train that would be bearing Carter, who she'd come to think of as her Sir Galahad, a dashing knight who would rescue her from her misery. It was a stupid dream, of course, and no matter what Maddie had said, totally unfair to expect of a fellow she barely knew. Still, they'd agreed to meet and talk. She was obliged to at least chat with him a bit, see how he maybe felt.

When he got off the train, she realized something was wrong. He seemed glad to see her, but there was a faraway look in his eyes whenever she was talking. His mind was, for sure, somewhere else, and not with her there on the Northwood platform. He made no move toward the station exit but stood in one spot as the train edged away.

"I was going to give you a summary of all me problems," said Fiona, "but I think you've got yourself a wee bit of trouble, too."

"No . . . yes . . . well, a bit. But let's not get into that. I'm sorry, something's come up so I don't have much time. Can we, like, sit over here and talk for a while? Then I can catch another train on home."

Fiona's heart sank. This was not going at all like she'd imagined. He'd seemed so disappointed that first time on the train when she said she'd not be seeing him again. And yesterday, he lit up like he'd won a million pounds when he saw her waiting with Maddie. But now, now he was like another person. *What have I done? What did I do?* She tried to think back to their short time in the *Cock and Crow*, and couldn't come up with anything that would lead to . . . this.

"You said yesterday you had problems," Carter said, wasting no time when they'd found an empty bench. "Let's hear it."

The brusque tone in Carter's voice made Fiona hesitate. Even when he'd been treating her like the Cinderella he'd been searching for all over the kingdom, she'd hesitated bringing her problems to him. Now with him acting like he had to be somewhere else, she definitely thought it would be a mistake.

Maybe if I just hint at me troubles a bit, that'd be enough. "I told ye I had two brothers, didn't I?"

"Yes. You seemed like you didn't want to talk about them, so I didn't ask."

"Well, I didn't, and I thank ye for not bein' pushy."

"But now?"

"Now I'd like to say a wee bit about them, but you stop me if I'm boring you or keeping you from whatever . . ."

"Hey, Fiona, if my problems were so important—more important than you—do you think I'd have gotten off that train?"

"I don't know. I'm just afraid to dump my things on you, be too much of a burden. Especially if you have your own . . ."

Carter was no longer staring into space. He'd turned to Fiona, taken one of her hands in both of his, and looked into her eyes.

"Look, I'm sorry I'm acting a bit strange. It's true, something's come up at home I have to take care of, but it's been going on for a long time. It can wait. I'm here . . ." He broke off suddenly, tilted his head, and smiled. "Your eyes, they're green. In the train, I thought they were brown, but here in the sunlight . . . they're really green. And they're . . ." Carter looked at his feet. ". . . beautiful."

Fiona felt her face flush. She'd been complimented about her eyes in the past, but this time was different. She struggled to come up with a reply. "Your hair is nice." She immediately knew that was the lamest thing she could have said and stammered trying to think of something better, but she finally gave up. Besides, Carter was laughing, not in a mean way, but still. . . . She started to chuckle, too. "That sounded a bit wanky, right?"

"I'm not sure what that means, but it must be true, if you say so." They both began to laugh again.

The next train rolled into the station, and both of them fell silent under the clanking and screeching sounds of tons of machinery heaving to a stop. Fiona didn't breathe, waiting to see if Carter would jump up and leave her there. He didn't.

When the train had rolled itself out of sight and out of earshot, Carter said, "All right. Now tell me about these brothers of yours that are giving you some kind of trouble."

"I don't . . ."

"And I want to hear everything, got it? Give me the whole story of what's bothering you. Look, I'm no psychological whiz kid, but

I know something about trouble. You keep it inside you, and it just eats away in there, until there's nothing of you left. Just a shell. You can't have those pretty green eyes of yours looking at the world out of a shell. I won't allow it."

"Oh, *you* won't allow it, is it? You've made yourself my psychiatrist, have you?"

"Damn right. Now, what about these brothers?"

After they left the Burlington Arcade, Sean Haverty took his charges back to the East London alley where they kept their bomb-making equipment. Haverty had obviously been there recently, because there was a small television set in the corner sitting on an upturned crate. "That's not for watchin' your Roadrunner cartoons, laddies, that's so you can see what's happening on our big day."

"How can we be watching the telly if we're over to Burlington Arcade doin' what we're there to be doin'?" asked Fergie.

"Good question," said Haverty. "Shows you're not totally brain dead. I told you I got three cells, A, B, C, right? Well, we're going to set off our bombs a couple of hours apart, not all at once. That's because Sean Haverty's goin' to be the one what sets them all off. And I gotta get from one place to the other."

"So you don't trust us to do it?"

"I seen guys freeze up at the last minute, seen all kinds of things they themselves didn't think was possible. So, yeah, I'm going to set off the bombs. You lads is going to *place* the bombs and do whatever it takes to keep 'em hidden till the right minute. Don't think that ain't important."

Gordie wanted to be somewhere else, but curiosity got the best of him. "You still didn't say why you put a telly in here, exactly."

"You boys are Cell B, right? But that don't mean you're gonna go second. You're gonna go third. I can't tell you where the other two are, but they're real close together, so they gotta both go before the idiots wake up and realize the first one wasn't what they call an 'isolated incident.' "

"Maddock said we was gonna be like a big windstorm," said Fergie. "Gonna blow these Brits clean off their island."

Haverty laughed. "Maybe old Maddock wasn't so stupid after all. That's right, we do three bombs in a row, bang bang bang, and they'll be cryin' for mercy. That's why the first two got to be pretty close to the same time."

"But won't they realize it's not an isolated incident then, before we do ours?" said Fergie. "Don't think I like that."

"That's just it. The first two targets are military. Yours is civilian, so they'll never suspect we'd be doing one there. They'd be all messing their britches trying to protect more military things. You just waltz in there easy as pork pie."

"And the telly?" Gordie was getting a little steamed because he wasn't getting an answer about the dumb television set.

"You watch the telly, and right after the second bomb goes off, you head for Burlington Arcade. I'll meet you there."

"What if it's not on telly?"

"Are you joking? This'll be on every television in the world, not just this one here. Don't you worry about that."

"How do we get to the Arcade?" said Fergie. "You want us to lug bombs across town on some London Underground train? That'd be stupid at any time, but right after two bombs have blown up your military targets?"

"Nah. I'll leave you a van you can load your things in and drive over to Burlington. Park right in front where the delivery vans stop. Then you load your 'deliveries' on a dolly and haul 'em inside, big-as-you-please. Act like you do it all the time, like it's the most natural thing in the world." Haverty grabbed his chin and cocked his head. "One a you *can* drive, can't you?"

Fergie, Gordie knew, had driven a bit around their uncle's Connemara farm, but he'd for sure never done it in a town, let alone a big city like London. Still, he could see Fergie was thinking hard about whether to volunteer he could, of course, drive the van. Then Paddy O'Brien spoke up and said, sure that he was able to do the drivin' and glad of it.

For the first time in his life, Gordie was thankful driving a car was a skill he'd never acquired.

"I think I deserve a round, don't you? One round for the successful conclusion of a grueling campaign."

"I might agree, Maddie, if I had even the slightest clue as to what campaign you are talking about." C.C. Piper raised her half-pint of shandy and took a sip.

"The lad. I found my young lad. I was able to do it without the help of my two good friends." She raised her glass toward each of them in turn. "But first, I found a girl, who was also looking for the boy who was, with the help of another boy, looking for the girl. I think I have that right."

Babs Kroome said, "Maddie, you don't need another round. In fact, from what I just heard, I think you've already had too much to drink." She reached over and took Maddie's mug and handed it to C.C.

Maddie reached across the table and took her drink back. "If I spoke too quickly for you, I certainly understand. The brain cells don't work quite as well at your ages as they once did."

She proceeded to recap the story of her search for the elusive Carter Chamberlain, the not-so-chance meeting with the Irish lassie, Fiona, and the amazing fact that Carter and Fiona had been looking for each other since that fateful day on the train when their paths had crossed. "Three paths, actually. Both young people and me."

"I suppose you consider yourself odd-woman-out, though," said C.C. "I'm quite sure the young ones will write their own agenda, one which likely does not include a certain woman. A woman of an advanced age."

"But very spry and youthful," said Babs, quickly.

"A woman of great charm," added C.C.

"A woman," said Maddie, "with a very strange taste in friends."

Chapter 16

THE DAY AFTER FIONA'S MEETING WITH Carter on the Northwood Station bench, she felt two very conflicting emotions. In one way, she felt a huge weight had been lifted from her, just because she'd shared her feelings with someone else. Carter had been absolutely right about that. On the other hand, as she told him about her brothers, she realized it was only her gut feeling made her think they were in serious trouble. She had no hard evidence, and had to admit that to Carter, and to herself.

In spite of the fact Carter obviously had some problems of his own to deal with, after they'd sat on the bench, he'd given her his full attention. He really seemed to want to know every detail, every fact, every thought, even those that were just vague feelings. He held her hand. He looked into her eyes. He seemed to be looking into the deepest part of her, and this was both thrilling and frightening. It was something so new in her life, she didn't know how to handle it—didn't know if she *could* handle it.

The chance to gain the hard evidence she wanted came that very evening. Fergie and Gordie gave her the usual dodgy excuses when they went out. They started in with, "Fancy a pint, Gordie?" followed by, "Oh, for sure now, Fergie. I've got me a throat on me." After that it was, "Think our gingernut sis can hold things down around the house while we toss a few darts?"

Naturally, they *did* think their redheaded sister would keep the house from burning down while they went out. That was her function in life. Nothing different there. But tonight, she was bound it would be different. She ran to her mother's room, made sure she was tucked in and sleeping, grabbed a sweater from her own room, and dropped it near the door where she could retrieve it in a hurry.

When the two brothers left the house, punching each other's shoulders and laughing about how each would beat the bejeezus out of the other at darts, Fiona slipped on her sweater and followed them at a distance.

Sure enough, they didn't head for their local pub, or any other beer-and-darts establishment. Instead, they went directly to the train station and bought a ticket. Thankful she had a few pounds in her pocketbook, she told the counterman she wanted a round-trip ticket to the same place as the two young men who'd just been there.

The counterman peered at her with a quizzical look. "Sure you wanta go to Stepney Green, this time a night, miss? Bit of a rough area after dark."

"'Course I do. I can take care a meself, don't you worry none." Inside she was trying to convince herself of that very thing.

Fiona poked her head through the door and saw her brothers on the platform to her left. They were watching the tracks, waiting for the train, not moving, not talking. *Just like I thought. All that shoving and laughing was for my benefit. Away from me they've gone dead serious.* She turned her head away from the brothers and hurried down the platform to her right, far enough to make sure she ended up in a different car than them, but not so far she'd lose them later.

The train they got on had doors with windows at the end of each car, so the ticket-taker could go from car to car. Fiona resisted the temptation to peer through the window into the car with her brothers, certain one of them would look up and see her. That wouldn't do at all. In a million years, she'd never think of an explanation that made sense.

She had a moment of panic at Baker Street Station. Her brothers got off the train and disappeared into a mass of people that seemed to be charging in every direction. The station had a maze of tunnels and passageways, some leading up, some down, and some very, very down. There were five different underground subway lines that crossed at Baker Street, and her brothers could be heading for any of them. She wished she had some idea of which Tube line went to Stepney Green, but she was clueless.

As she was about to give up, she saw Fergie's dark green windbreaker rounding a corner where a sign read "Hammersmith and City." She rushed to close the gap and just managed to get to the Hammersmith platform in time to see her brothers getting onto a train that had just arrived. She ran for the nearest door, which was already starting to close. An older man shoved a worn briefcase into the gap, and the doors opened back up.

"Little trick I learned, long ago. Of course, my briefcase *is* a bit worse for the wear."

"I thank ye very much, sir," Fiona managed to say, between gasps for breath. She rubbed her face and smiled, "And please tell your briefcase I'm right sorry if I caused it more grief."

"My dear girl, I know for a fact, my briefcase is overjoyed to be of service. He lives to help young ladies in distress."

Fiona was so tired from running after her brothers, she settled back in a seat and watched the other passengers. Some few were business types, but as they went along, the most of them were working stiffs. More than a few gave Fiona a look, and some of those looks were downright vulgar. She tried to ignore the leering and the toothy grins by closing her eyes.

She woke up with a start. The train was stopped, and she could see a sign through the window that read *Stepney Green*.

"Crickey." Fiona jumped to her feet and bolted for the door. Again, it was starting to close, and this time there was no overjoyed briefcase to come to her rescue. *What the heck.* She stuck a foot in the doorway and waited to see if it would get lopped off or serve as a makeshift briefcase. Thankfully, the fates and the London Underground engineers were kind. The doors opened for a brief second and she slipped through, remembering at the last minute that she was making a spectacle of herself. If her brothers were exiting past her door, she was cooked.

They weren't. The few people leaving the train at Stepney Green were almost all partway up the escalator. No sign of Fergie and Gordie. They must already be at the top and on their way outside. *Double crickey.* When she reached the street, she looked in vain for her brothers. It was getting dark now, and the street disappeared in both directions into the gloom. Worse, there were intersections nearby that led off to who-knows-how-many places. There was no way to know which way to go. She started to take a chance on the street that seemed to have the most light, but then changed her mind. *If there's light, I should oughta see them and I don't.*

It was almost an hour before Fiona managed to reverse her journey and climb wearily up the McKenna front steps. She had stopped crying halfway home, but the tears of frustration were now back. Inside, she threw down her sweater and searched frantically in her pocketbook for the little slip of paper where Carter Chamberlain had written his phone number. Still sobbing, she took a quick look at her sleeping mother, and then sank heavily onto a kitchen chair. After a minute she cried out without making a sound, and reached for the telephone.

Carter was almost afraid to go into the house. Day before yesterday, he'd been greeted by a little sister who was crying in fear and pain and guilt that maybe she had caused their mother's outburst. It had taken all the brotherly advice and gentle talk he could muster to calm her down. She'd slept well enough and seemed almost okay in the morning, so he took her to the bus stop and waited until she'd headed off to school.

Even though he had to take the train into St. John's Wood every day, Amy had an even longer commute, by bus, to an international school in a converted old mansion out in the country. He'd been there once, when they were getting Amy registered, and it was an incredible place. Huge old house with hardwood floors and stained glass windows and a spooky basement, which kids could pretend was haunted. Unfortunately, they didn't "do" high school, so he had to ride the friggin' train into London.

ASL turned out to be a pretty cool place, too, but he'd had a devil of a time trying to make up for arriving near the end of term. They were in their last week before summer vacation, and he still had five tough finals to bone up on. As he turned the key in the lock, he took a deep breath. *Please let there be peace tonight. I need some quiet time.*

The house was silent. Maybe too silent. Carter checked his watch. He'd spent enough time in the library after school so Amy *ought* to be home. He crept back to his parents' room and peered in. Mom was in bed, sleeping. This time her bathrobe was in place, and she'd been covered with a light blanket. Carter checked the rest of the house. No Amy. He guessed maybe her bus was just late. He'd give it another hour before he got worried.

He started to fix himself a snack to go with his Chemistry and English and History books. He had a ton of work ahead. When he was getting out some corn flakes, he noticed something behind the cereal boxes. It was an unopened bottle of Gilbey's gin. *Damn.* He wondered how many bottles she had stashed around the house. He decided the studying could wait a few more minutes, so he started rummaging through cupboards and drawers, and peering under furniture. He found two more bottles, one gin, one vodka, and another half-full bottle of Canadian whisky. He drained them all in the kitchen sink and threw the empties into the rubbish bin outside.

By the time he'd finished that little chore, he was beginning to get worried about Amy again. It was hard to concentrate on his books, and all the things he knew for absolute sure were going to be on the tests he hadn't been around to learn earlier. He'd always been proud of the grades he managed to wangle with a lot of hard work. How would it look now, just one more year before college, if he slipped badly. No, he just couldn't let it happen. *C'mon, Carter. Just two more days. Three finals tomorrow and two the next day. You can do it.* Truth was, he wasn't so sure. Maybe, if there were no more distractions. Maybe.

He heard the front door open and heard Amy's voice. She sounded fine. *Thank God.* Then he heard a man's voice and jumped to see who it was.

"Dad! What are you doing home? You never get home this early."

"Hi, son. Just stopped by to get some things. Gotta go on a little trip."

"Where? Where are you going?"

"Just a business trip. Well, a little more than a trip. I have a new assignment. Gonna mean a bit of travel."

"How much travel?"

"Oh, just some. A week now and then. Two or three at the most. It's a great opportunity. I'll be servicing accounts in Brussels and Vienna and Paris. All kinds of neat places. Great opportunity."

Carter choked. "What about Mom? What about Amy? Don't you think they need to have? . . ."

"What about me? Don't you think I deserve a nice promotion? I'd think you'd be happy for me." He didn't wait for an answer, but stalked off to the bedroom. Carter could hear him hauling luggage down off the shelf and the clinking of clothes hangers as he pulled things out of the closet. Carter went to the bedroom door and watched the man he called Dad. He had laid his clothes on the bed, directly on top of his mother. One by one he was picking them up, folding them, and packing them neatly into a suitcase lying open on the floor.

Carter couldn't help himself. "That's your *wife* there. That lump under the covers is your friggin' *wife*."

Dad stopped for a moment, but he didn't look at Carter. He started packing again, a little faster now, a little sloppier.

"That's right. Don't say a damn thing, Daddy Dear. Mom'll get along without you. Amy'll get along without you, and I know darn well I'll get along just fine without you." Carter stalked back to the kitchen. Amy was sitting at the table, staring at the doorway, when Carter entered. He kneeled and put his arms around her.

"I know you heard that, Kitten. I know. But don't worry. Everything will be just fine. I'm going to make Mommy all better, and Daddy will be back before you know it. It's going to be fine, Kitten. Listen to your big brother. Everything's gonna be okay."

Carter picked up a textbook on European History 1200–1943. He started to open it, but then he threw it hard on the table. "Make yourself a snack, Kitten. I need to think a minute." But his thoughts were disjointed, random. He couldn't seem to process everything and put it into logical order. He knew he needed to put first things first. He knew he'd be overwhelmed if he didn't start working on them one-at-a-time. But what was first? He held his face in both hands to protect his little sister from the misery he knew was flooding out of every pore on his face.

He was in that position when the phone rang. He picked it up and heard an anguished female voice cry, "Oh, Carter. Oh, Carter, I need you." Before he had a chance to choke out a reply, he knocked his History book crashing to the floor, the front door slammed, and Amy burst into tears.

Chapter 17

THE NEXT TWO DAYS WERE SURREAL. Carter had used the half of his mind not obsessing with family to listen to Fiona's tale about following and losing her brothers in Stepney Green. Once again they'd agreed to meet in a neutral place, a bench beside the tracks at Northwood Station. Fiona was now absolutely certain they were in some sort of trouble, but still had no idea what. "It's bad, though, Carter. I feel it. It's bad."

While she talked, Carter's mind was starting to clear, just a bit. He was trying to figure out his priorities so he could come up with *some* kind of plan. A strange thought popped into his mind. He remembered a quote from Oscar Wilde that went something like, *You have to distinguish the truly important from the merely urgent.* He decided it was a weird time to be thinking of famous quotations when a frantic girl was pouring her heart out and asking for help. But it made sense. Of all the things piling up on his plate, what things were most important?

Amy, first. His Kitten was number one, for sure.

Mom, next. Getting her fixed maybe wasn't all that urgent, but it sure as heck was important.

After that, getting through this school year. He'd invested eleven years of his life to get to this spot, and it would be stupid to blow his future at this stage of the game.

Then Fiona's brothers. He felt bad, really bad, putting off helping Fiona find out what was going on with her brothers, but how urgent could it be? Surely, learning what they were up to could wait a couple of days, till school was over.

He told her, "I didn't tell you much the other day, but I've got stuff here at home that needs my attention. Still, I really want to hear more about your brothers. Help you figure out what to do. Suppose you can come to my house tomorrow night?" He had another thought. "After supper. Come after supper."

Fiona had finally talked her way out of her fits of crying. She barely sniffed when she agreed to come. Carter insisted she write down the directions. His mind was working again.

He was up till almost 1:00 A.M. studying, and in the morning he studied some more on the train through heavy-lidded eyes. Later, he had no clear idea how he did on his final exams. The one in English was probably all right; they didn't seem to be learning anything he hadn't had before. History was another thing—all those facts that needed to be memorized. He probably screwed that one up pretty good. Algebra—who knows?

All the way home he worried about how stupid it had been to invite Fiona over. How would his mother act? Since he'd taken away her stash of booze, she probably wouldn't be passed out in her room. How would she be? Like a druggie suffering withdrawal pains, or what? Of course, Fiona said her own mum had been a basket case since her husband got killed, but Carter was still embarrassed his mother was an alcoholic, and an emotional wreck to boot.

It worked out even worse than he feared.

Not at first, though. When Fiona arrived, Carter's mom was safely tucked away in her bedroom. Fiona was standing with her head bowed when he opened the door, but when she looked up and saw Carter, her face brightened and she smiled like there was nothing bad anywhere in the world. He instantly forgot all his own troubles, reached for her hand, and led her inside. He wanted to wrap his arms around her but decided that would be pushing it. Or maybe not. Either way, she would have to make the first move.

"Okay," he said, when they'd settled side-by-side on the couch, "you said you went by yourself to London, a seedy area in East London. After dark. Are you crazy?"

"I needed to know where me brothers were goin', all secret like. But then I lost them."

"Because it was dark, I imagine."

"I couldn't help that. Couldn't order them to go in the daytime so as I could secretly follow them in the light, could I now?"

"Guess not. But you should have taken somebody with you."

"And who would that be? I haven't had a school chum ever since I dropped outta school, and you know what me mum's like."

Carter wanted to say, *Me, of course. You should have asked me!* But he knew full well he would have told her he needed to wait a few days until his own school year was over. In fact, that was still the case. In his order of important things to do, worrying about Fiona's brothers had come in fourth. Somehow, he had to stall her without actually saying that.

What he did say surprised the both of them. "I told you I was setting myself up to be a detective, when I was trying to find you. I would have done it, too, as soon as school's over. And last day's tomorrow, by the way. So, what I'll do is, instead of looking for *you*, I'll look for your brothers. Oughta be a piece a cake."

"But I'm goin' with you."

"Nah. I'm thinking I could probably wander around East London easier without you. You'd have every bozo in the area staring at that head of red hair."

Fiona laughed. "Not to mention my green eyes, which someone told me are quite fetching."

"People do say things. Listen, there's someone I want you to meet." He jumped up and ran down the hallway. A moment later he was back with his sister in hand.

"Amy. This is the girl I told you about. This is Fiona. Fiona, this is my best girl, Amy."

Amy looked a bit embarrassed but she stuck out a small hand, and Fiona gave it a good shake. "I am so happy to be meetin' with you, Amy. Your brother has told me a good many nice things about ye."

"I'm . . . I'm happy to meet you, too."

Carter said, "Fiona and I have some really important things to discuss, Kitten, but I wanted you to meet her. Whatcha doing in your room? Bunch a tough homework?"

Amy laughed and shook her head. "Nooo. I'm making a collage with magazine pictures."

"Sounds like loads of fun," said Carter. "I'll be in later to see what you made."

When Amy had left, Carter said, "Now, where were we?"

Fiona's face turned serious. She said, "I don't see how you're going to do it. You can't stand at Stepney Green Station every day till they show up. Besides, you don't even know what they look like."

"Ah, but do you think the great Sherlock Holmes would have been deterred by such trivia?"

"What?"

Carter was starting to tell her about the modern-day Sherlock Holmes Detective Agency he and Josh Weaver planned, when they heard a phlegmy cough from the bedroom door. "What the heck is going on here? Who are you?" Carter's mother was pointing a shaky finger at Fiona.

Carter spoke first. "This is Fiona McKenna, Mom. A friend."

"Yeah, right. My husband had a 'friend' in Houston looked a lot like you. Hustling slutty little bi . . ."

"Mom. Can it. Fiona is a friend, nothing more. Why don't you go read something, have a nice bath? You'll feel better after a nice, relaxing . . ."

"I'd feel better if my thieving son hadn't gone around the house stealing things. Things didn't belong to him."

Fiona stood up. "Maybe I best be goin' on me way."

"No. You sit, Fiona." Carter waved her down. "No one's going to kick *my* friends out of *my* house."

"I'm the mother here. You're the kid, and don't you forget it. Since when have you earned one damn nickel to pay for the rent of this place?"

"Since when have you? How long's it been since you did *anything* around here? Fixed a meal for Amy? Washed a dish or any other of your wifely duties?"

Nelda Chamberlain screeched and ran at her son, flailing her fists. Carter jumped to the side and fell against Fiona, who had settled back cowering on the couch. By the time he'd found his feet again, his mother had run from the room, screaming incoherently. He could hear her slamming kitchen cupboard doors. There was a huge crash as what sounded like a drawer full of silverware crashed to the floor. Carter was torn between trying to wrestle his mother out of the kitchen or comforting the girl who was now crying uncontrollably on his living room couch. He chose to stay.

This time, he didn't hesitate a bit. He sat beside Fiona, put his arms around her, and pulled her to him. She stiffened at first and then went limp against him. They stayed that way, listening to the symphony of noise move from the kitchen to the laundry room. After what sounded like soap boxes thudding to the floor, it got quiet. A moment later Carter's mom walked into the living room and gave her son a sour look that seemed to say, *take that*. She didn't slow down but headed straight for the door to the bedrooms. In her hand she was carrying a bottle of something brown. As she got to the doorway, she turned back with a crooked smile and lifted the bottle like she was giving a toast.

After a long period of silence, Carter said, "I'm sorry you had to see that."

Fiona pulled away from him and touched his face with the back of her hand. "I'm only sorry there was something like that for me to see."

Chapter 18

THE FOLLOWING DAY WAS THE LAST DAY of school. In prior years, Carter would have spent every possible minute seeking out friends, trying to outdo each other in bad-mouthing teachers or joking about how lazy their summers were going to be. This one was different. Almost no part of his brain was engaged in anything dealing with the American School in London. He navigated the last two finals on cruise control, barely conscious of the questions or the answers he gave.

Much of his mind was filled with the four-step program he'd set for himself—Amy, Mom, school, Fiona. He was already shuffling the order of things in his mind. Not that the order of importance had changed. It was just that one of the "merely" urgent things wasn't so "merely." He had to use the last day of school to set things in motion for finding the secret of Fiona's brothers. He needed to reestablish the Twentieth Century Sherlock Holmes Detective Agency. And for that, he needed to re-employ his sidekick Josh (Watson) Weaver.

"So what are you doing Monday, Weaver?"

"Guess I'll probably sleep till about two in the afternoon. Then I'll have lunch and take a nap."

"Seems like a really bad way to earn that camping trip. The Scottish Highlands. Mmm. Mmm."

"What're you on about? You found your hotty, or miracle-of-miracles, she found you."

"Different job. Different mystery. Ooooo . . ."

Fiona still didn't understand how Carter could possibly find Fergie and Gordie's destination in East London without her going along. He didn't even know what they looked like! True, he'd asked for pictures, but she'd scoured the house for hours, looking for something that wasn't years old. He'd told her not to worry. He had a plan for that. *Right, not to worry. What else am I supposed to do? Take up knitting?*

Saturday morning, she decided to confront him with her concerns and beg him again to let her go with him to Stepney Green. She phoned his home and heard a sleepy female voice. Inwardly, she cursed, but tried to sound as cheerful as possible. "Good morning, Mrs. Chamberlain. Might I speak with Carter, please?"

It seemed like a rather straightforward request, answerable by either, "I'll go get him," or "Afraid the lazy bum's still in bed. I'll have him call you." Instead she got total silence, long enough for her to say, "Mrs. Chamberlain? Ma'am, are you there? Is this the right number?"

Finally, the voice answered. The sleepiness was gone, replaced by a hard edge, each word standing alone. "This may be the number you want, but it is most certainly *not* the *right* number. Not for you, missy."

"But . . . but, Mrs. Chamberlain, how can you know who I am, or what I want?"

"I know exactly who you are. You're the little hussy who was curling herself all over my son. You're the red-haired little . . ."

"Just a minute, Mrs. Chamberlain." Fiona suddenly found a touch of courage she didn't know was in her. "I'm sorry your husband had a fling with some redhead, but I'm not that person. And let me tell you this. Carter is *not* your husband. He's your son."

"Yes, and I'm his mother. And his mother is warning you to stay away."

Fiona phoned the Chamberlain home three more times during the day. Twice she hung up without speaking when she heard the raspy female voice, but not before the voice turned into an almost-incoherent screech. It wasn't until the third call she heard Carter's quiet "Hello?"

"Oh, Carter, I've been trying the whole day, but . . . can you talk?"

"I'm alone, if that's what you mean."

"Are you still . . . do you still want to help? Find where me brothers go?"

"Absolutely. My detective agency is at your complete disposal."

"Ohhh, silly."

"Please, madam, you cut me to the bone. You have no . . ."

"I'm going."

"What?"

"Going with you and your entire detective agency. To Stepney Green. And that's that."

"No, that's *not* that. Listen, I'm meeting Maddie and her friends at her pub this afternoon. To celebrate my getting through the school year, she said. Why don't you meet us? *Cock and Crow*, Rickmansworth, five o'clock."

"If it's all right with the great detective for me to leave my house."

"Rickmansworth at 5:00 P.M. is a little different than Stepney Green after dark."

"But it's not me whose honor is at risk," said Fiona, in a dramatic voice. "According to your mother, *you* are the one whose virtue may be lost."

Carter was stumped. He couldn't think of a thing to say.

Maddie and her two friends were already at the *Cock and Crow* when Carter got there. It seemed to him like maybe they'd been there for a while. He watched them from the doorway for a minute so his eyes could adjust to being out of the bright sunlight. They laughed at something Maddie said, were quiet for a few seconds while another of the ladies spoke, then took off cackling again. Seemed like an awful lot of laughing for so few words.

He approached their table quietly and stood until one of the ladies looked up and raised her mug.

"Speak of the devil, here he is."

Carter started to speak, but another of the trio interrupted. "Now, now, Babs. This might not be our boy at all."

"Nonsense, C.C. How many other gorgeous young men do you suppose there are around here? Ones who will stand there looking all bashful in front of a gaggle of old geese like us?"

Madeleine Westfall had her hands over her eyes, and she was heaving with laughter. Finally, she managed to choke out, "Yes, girls. This is our young man."

Carter looked back quickly toward the doorway, then stepped forward and held out his hand. For a brief second, he was afraid it was bad form for a man to initiate a handshake with a woman, but the one who was called C.C. grabbed his hand and shook it vigorously. "Do forgive us for our rudeness. We've been at the shandy for a few minutes."

"Oh, C.C.," said Babs. "Only a minute. Don't give him the idea we're a bunch of lushes."

"Better he think we've tippled a bit than to think we're just naturally barmy."

Maddie stood up and led Carter to an empty chair. "Please pay no attention to my friends. They really are good sorts even if they are, as C.C. says, a bit barmy."

After introductions, C.C. said, "You keep looking at the door, Carter. I don't blame you for wanting to escape."

"No. No. It's not that. I asked someone to meet us here." He nodded toward Maddie. "You remember Fiona."

"Oh, that's wonderful. A lovely girl. So are the two of you? . . ."

"She wants me to help her do something, and she wants to go with me when I do it, and . . . oh, it's complicated. I thought maybe you could listen to her story and maybe help talk some sense into her. I think I know what's right, but I just . . . well, I thought maybe you . . ."

"You think I'm old and wise."

Carter stammered, "No. No. Not old, just . . ."

"Wise?"

"Exactly."

"Is that your Fiona in the doorway?"

Carter leaped to his feet and ran to the door. A moment later, he returned with a bashful-looking girl by the hand. Fiona brightened when she saw Maddie Westfall and gave a small curtsy.

After another round of introductions, Maddie waved to the woman who was waiting tables as well as tending bar. "My friends and I will have another round of shandies, Helen, and see what our two young friends will have." To Carter she said, "Their house lager is excellent."

"I told you at the station, I don't drink."

"I know about the drinking age in your United States, but in the United Kingdom, a lad your age can partake of beer or cider, providing it is served with a meal. Helen, we'd best have something to eat. Can you? . . ."

"I didn't say I *can't* drink. I said I *don't* drink. That means I *won't* drink."

"I'm sorry, Carter, I didn't mean to upset you."

Carter sat staring at the table. Finally, he looked up, gave Maddie a weak smile and said, "You have what you want, Fiona. Don't pay any attention to me."

Fiona shook her head. "I'll have whatever Carter has, if you please."

They settled on Cokes and sat quietly for a few minutes. All the laughter Carter interrupted had vanished like the foam on a mug of beer.

Maddie said Carter wanted to discuss a problem Fiona was having, and obtain the opinion of a "wise old owl, such as myself."

Fiona looked startled and started to jump up. Carter put his hand on her arm and eased her back down. "I'm sorry I sprung this on you. I just don't see you and me agreeing on this thing about your going to Stepney Green. I just thought Maddie could help."

After several more minutes of coaxing, interrupted by the arrival of their drinks, Fiona finally said, "I suppose it won't kill me to air me dirty laundry in public."

After she got started, she gradually lost her reluctance until finally she'd laid out the whole story. All three ladies gasped when they heard about the killing of Fiona's father in Belfast, at the hands of Protestant extremists. They cupped their mouths and said, "oh, my!" and "dear me," at the plight of Fiona's mother, who had been out of touch with reality for six years. They clucked sympathetically when Fiona described how care of their mother had fallen almost entirely to her. When she expressed fear at what her brothers may be up to, making clandestine trips to East London, they didn't say a word.

There was a moment of silence, then Carter spoke up. "So, there's our problem. I need to find out where in Stepney Green Fiona's brothers go and what they do there. She insists she go with me, and I won't have it. It's a rough neighborhood after dark, and it won't just put her in danger, she'll make it harder for me to do . . . what I have to do."

Maddie said, "Yes, I see your problem. You have something of a stalemate here."

"Right. I want to help. I really do. But I won't do it if she tags along. Simple as that."

"I think," said Maddie, "this situation calls for a compromise. Something you can both live with."

"I dunna see what that might be," said Fiona. "Our Carter, here, seems a wee bit stubborn."

"And you're not?"

Maddie waved both of her hands. "The nature of compromise is to discover something comfortable to both parties. I've been thinking, and I've come up with a perfect solution. Fiona will go with you to Stepney Green, but will stay inside the station while you go about your business."

"Uh, uh. That's even worse. I don't want her alone, hanging around a deserted train station in East London. No way."

"But here is the beauty of the plan, She won't be alone. She'll be chaperoned by a very matronly looking older lady. I know Babs and C.C. will understand my plan perfectly." After they had nodded their approval, Maddie added, "Fiona will have an ideal bodyguard. Me."

Carter had read about a fairly recent invention they were calling a "mobile cellular" telephone. The beauty of the thing was you could go almost anywhere and talk to someone at home or someone with another mobile cellular phone. It would have been a perfect way for them to keep each other advised about when Fiona's brothers left the house, got on the train, and so on. Only problems were, they didn't work everywhere, they cost an arm and a leg, and he didn't know a soul that actually had one of the things.

The Modern Sherlock Holmes Detective Agency was forced to operate the old-fashioned way, much like the original Sherlock. Fiona would try to anticipate when the brothers planned their next getaway and phone Carter at home, so he could hightail it to Northwood Station in time to be on the same train with the brothers and, of course, with Maddie and Fiona. Josh lived closer to downtown London, so he would have time to get to Stepney Green before the others.

The only possible problem was the need for Fiona to get past the gatekeeper, Carter's mother. If Mom answered the phone, Carter would never hear "the caper is afoot." They decided

Fiona would call Maddie, who would call Carter, claiming to be a secretary from the American School in London, needing to talk to Carter about some papers. Maddie said, "I'm normally against lying, but a modicum of deception can be tolerated, if the cause is just."

Carter said, "I'm not sure how much a 'modicum' is, but it sure seems like a good thing to me."

Fiona said, "I *do* know what a 'modicum' is, unlike our American friend, and I know darn well it's something needs doing."

They didn't have to wait long for action. On Monday afternoon, Fergie and Gordie started fidgeting around the house, picking things up and laying them down without using them. Fiona had come to realize this nervousness was a clear sign they were planning a trip to the pub for "a couple a pints and some darts." She called Maddie and "set the caper afoot." The weather was pleasant, but she decided to lay her sweater casually by the door anyway, since they might be out in the night air for hours. At almost exactly 6:00 P.M., the boys made their lame excuses and paraded out the door arm-in-arm, two mates out for a bit of fun. Fiona told them she planned to "read me a good book, and catch a few winks." She didn't feel even a modicum of regret about the lie. She kissed her mother, grabbed her sweater, and hurried after her lying brothers.

When Maddie made her phone call, Carter answered, so there was no need to invent a story about ASL paperwork. He ran around the house, collecting some things he might need. Some notepaper and a pencil, a flashlight, and a half-dozen candy bars went into a backpack. He figured they might need a little energy if they were on a long stakeout.

He stuck his head into Amy's room and asked her how she was doing. She said she was fine. "Why?"

"'Cause I have to go out for a while. Maybe for quite a while. So you'll have to tuck yourself into bed tonight."

"Mom's been making funny noises again."

"I know, Kitten, but you'll be fine if you stay in your room."

"What if she starts throwing things?"

"Stay in your room. Got it?"

Amy sniffled a bit, then nodded. Carter kissed the top of her head and headed out. Halfway down the block he changed his mind and turned back. On the far side of their house was a public footpath that went between their property and the people's next door. If he took the path, he could cut across some fields, go along a small creek, circle behind the soccer fields of a girls' school and cut a good five minutes off the trip to the station.

Maddie Westfall felt like a teenage girl, heading out of the house on a wild adventure. It was silly, of course, but that was the way of it. Silly or not, she was bound to enjoy whatever was about to happen. Instead of waiting for Carter at the station, she decided to walk toward his house and meet him halfway. There was only one reasonable route between house and station, so she felt no concern about passing him by mistake.

The longer she walked, the less sure she was she'd made a wise decision. Up ahead she could see the home Carter had shown her Saturday after their meeting at the *Cock and Crow*. Still no Carter, but she could see some sort of commotion in front of his house. As she neared, she saw a young girl crying uncontrollably. A woman wearing a pink dress and a kitchen apron was trying to console her, and several other people were standing in doorways watching. A young man rushed over to help the lady with the child. Maddie thought for a moment it was Carter, but the boy was shorter and stockier.

"What's the problem?" Maddie asked, when she reached the woman still trying to control the frantic little girl.

"It's that American woman," said the pink-dress lady. "She's frightened her little daughter something awful."

"Amy? Is this Carter's sister, Amy?"

The little girl stopped bawling when Maddie spoke, gave a couple of deep, choking gulps, and stared at Maddie with her mouth open.

"You are Amy, aren't you?"

The little girl nodded, then turned back toward the open door of her house and started crying again. A woman was leaning against the door jam, holding a bottle like a weapon, and wobbling back and forth. It was obvious to Maddie the woman was so completely drunk, it was a wonder she could stand up.

"You getcher fithy hands aw my dotter," she shouted, slurring her words so they barely made sense.

The pink lady said, "Listen to her. A woman like that has no business with a child. Frightened her to death, she has. I heard her myself, throwing things about, when the girl came running out the door in tears. Throwing and cursing and—well, it's a wonder the little girl hasn't been badly hurt."

"Or killed," added the young man. Several people inhaled dramatically at that announcement. They'd come down from their porches and were milling about on the lawn, looking grim, but clearly enjoying the spectacle, in Maddie's opinion.

She took Amy's hand and led her a few steps away from the pink lady. "I know this family. I can handle it from here."

"Too late," said one of the neighbors. "We've already called the coppers. They'll take care of things."

Maddie groaned inwardly. This was turning from a bad dream into a total nightmare. *Oh, where, oh, where is Carter?* Since she hadn't met him on the road, he must still be at home. Somewhere in that house behind that incoherent, drunken woman who has to be his mother. *Poor boy. Oh, please, please, let him be all right.* She had a brief vision of him lying on the floor, bleeding from a head wound inflicted by a bottle of whiskey.

Maddie was about to brave the threatening bottle and force her way into the house, when she heard the sound of sirens approaching. She decided to let the police subdue Mrs. Chamberlain, assuming that was who it was, and she would follow them into the house. Her mind flashed to Fiona, trying to avoid detection from her brothers at the train station. *What will she think when Carter and I don't show up?* Then she glanced again at little Amy and decided Fiona's problem was the least of it.

Carter paced the platform waiting for Maddie to show. *If a train comes, do I go? Or wait for another one? Where the heck is she?* He knew Maddie lived much closer to the station than he did. *Even an old lady shouldn't take this long to get ready.* He checked the schedule and saw that trains heading in to London at this time of day were, like, forty-five minutes apart. If he missed one, that would for sure be the one that would be picking up Fiona and her brothers in Northwood. No, the first train in, he'd have to take.

It was less than ten minutes later when a southbound train rolled in. Still no Maddie. With a final look at the empty doorway of the station ticket office, he shrugged and hopped on board. During the short ride to Northwood, he was trying to work out a strategy for handling Fiona. He stood watching the platform as they rolled into the station. Sure enough, there were the pair he assumed were Fiona's brothers, Fergie and Gordie, and there, hiding in the doorway, was Fiona herself, keeping one eye on the boys and one scanning the train windows.

When the doors opened, he rushed to intercept her, pushing her back into the ticket office. "Maddie's not coming, and neither are you." He pointed to a bench and said, "Sit there." Without waiting for an answer, he rushed back to the train and just managed to jump inside before the doors closed. The minute he got inside, he realized he was in the same car with the two brothers. Not only that, they were only a couple of feet away when he crashed into the side of some seats. One of the brothers, the older one, said, "Watch it, mate. Must be in a wee bit o' a hurry."

Carter smiled and looked for an empty seat. The doors opened briefly as another man managed to stick a foot in the gap, then sauntered on board like he didn't have a care in the world. Carter was still a bit breathless from his mad dash, and upset he could have saved himself the trouble.

Fiona barely touched the seat Carter had ordered her to sit in, before she was back on her feet following him. Her heart sank when she saw the doors start to close. She stopped and hung her head until she realized the man directly behind Carter had stuck his foot in the door. *Like me last train ride all over again.* As the doors opened again, she realized she had time to scurry down to the next car and get inside with no problem. She knew Carter would be snortin' angry with her, but there was no help for that. *Them's me own brothers, and it's me own decision, Carter Chamberlain.* She nodded her head, twice. *And that's that.*

Chapter 19

GORDIE MCKENNA SAT STILL AND STARED into his lap. Fergie was fidgety and nervous, tapping his foot and drumming his fist on his knee. Gordie thought it ought to be the other way around. He was the one who should be nervous. Sure-of-himself Fergie ought to be calm. Strange how the mind works. It wasn't that he, Gordie, was calm inside. Truth is, he was terrified—and disgusted with what he was about to do. Of course, Fergie was right. The rotten Brits did need to get out of Northern Ireland and let the good Catholic people live their lives without fear of getting killed by some crazy Protestant sniper. And the Irish had talked themselves blue in the face trying to convince the British to leave. No luck. So there was nothing left but to hit them where it would hurt the most, right here in their big fancy London.

Halfway up the escalator at Stepney Green Station, Fergie said, "You know, funny thing. I saw someone looked just like our sister back there."

Gordie stared down toward the platform. "I don't see no one."

"I don't, neither. Guess I'm just imaginin' things."

"You're probably thinking about her because we keep lying to her and then leaving her to take care a Mum."

"She likes to take care a Mum, don'tcha know? That's what girls is meant to do."

Carter adjusted his backpack and watched the two brothers go up the escalator in front of him. He didn't dare let them get too far ahead, because he remembered what happened to Fiona when she'd tried the same thing. He hurried after them, all the while whipping his head around looking for Josh. There he was, with his back to the white-tiled wall, looking cool. He nodded to Carter and fell into step. On the escalator, he said, "I saw two guys who looked right. That them?"

"They're just heading out the door, I'm guessing. We gotta hurry or we'll lose 'em."

When they got to the street, they saw the brothers trudging off to the right. Luckily, they didn't seem to be hurrying.

"We can follow 'em easy if they stay on streets with a light every once in a while."

"Piece a cake," said Josh.

"But there are lots of streets without lights," said a feminine voice.

Carter and Josh whipped around to find the source.

"Oh, hell," said Carter.

"Watch your language," said the feminine voice. "You must be Josh. In case you didn't figure it out, I'm Fiona. And I'm not supposed to be here, according to the Master."

Josh stammered a reply, and not too successfully. Carter said, "I never said you couldn't come. I just said if you insisted on coming, then I wouldn't. Big difference."

"But here I am, and here you are. Isn't this amazing, Josh? The Master's plans have gone astray. Whatever do we do about it? Hmm?"

Josh had recovered something approximating a voice. He said, "If we let your brothers out of sight, there'll be no reason for any of us to be here."

"You follow them," said Carter. "I'll stay here with this female person and try to figure out what to do with her. When they've gone inside somewhere, hightail it back and get me."

"Us," said Fiona.

After Josh had gone, Carter said, "Look, I've got to make a couple of phone calls. Find out what happened to Maddie and check on my sister. You stay right by my side. Think you can keep out of trouble?"

"If I had a leash, I'd let you fasten it to my collar and lead me to the phone booth."

Maddie's phone rang and rang. No answer. "Well, nothing we can do about it now." He paced back and forth for a moment, then said, "Now I gotta call home. I've been worrying about my sister. Mom was—well, just say she wasn't in good shape to take care of Amy. I need to see how things are."

On the third ring, someone answered, "Hello?"

Carter was puzzled. He said, "Maybe I dialed the wrong number. Is this the Chamberlain residence?"

The voice said, "Carter, is that you? Oh, I've been so worried. This is Maddie."

"Maddie? I don't understand. What are you doing there? Why aren't you here—I mean, why—Maddie, what's going on?"

"I would prefer to tell you about it when you get home. How is your quest?"

"We just got here. Fiona came, even though I specifically told her not to, I mean I told her I wouldn't come if she did."

"But . . ."

"But she came anyway. So she and me, we're at Stepney Green Station, and Josh is by himself trailing the brothers. I can't leave until he gets back."

"Quite right. There've been enough missed connections for one evening. You needn't rush back. I have things well under control here."

"Is Amy? . . ."

"Amy is fine. You're not to worry a bit."

"Thank God."

"Of course. There's no hurry, but—but don't start anything new."

Josh was back in less than an hour. "I know where they went. Looks like some warehouse or something. Middle of a dark alley."

"Could you see inside?"

"Nah. Couple of solid doors that slide up like on a garage. And one small door. No window in that, either."

"Then what?"

"Then nothing. Well, not exactly nothing. I could see some other guy coming down the alley with the streetlight behind him, so I took off the other way."

"This guy, did he? . . ."

"Dunno. He didn't come out the other end of the alley, so he might've gone to the same place, but who knows?"

Fiona said, "That's all well and good, Josh, but how are we to find this place next time we come a-lookin'?"

"Simple, dear lady. A clever detective such as myself will have no problem. The solution is 757."

"757?"

"Correct. 757."

"What the heck does 757 mean?" said Carter.

"That, my good Sherlock, is the number stenciled onto the door."

Fiona insisted she go home with Carter until they learned from Maddie what had happened. The front door was locked, and he rang the bell. Almost immediately, he heard Maddie's voice, "Who—who is it?" To Carter, she sounded hesitant, almost frightened.

"Me, Carter."

Maddie opened the door a crack and peered out. Then she threw the door open, grabbed Carter by the shoulders, and then hugged him. He was embarrassed but tried not to show it. When she finally let him go, he said, "Maddie, what's going on? You're acting like I came back from the dead or something."

"When I first arrived, I thought you . . . well, never mind that. You're here and all is well. Almost."

"What do you mean, almost?"

It wasn't until then Maddie noticed Fiona, standing at the bottom of the steps. She said, "Oh, Fiona, dear. So good you are here with Carter." Maddie motioned them into the living room. Amy was curled up on the couch, asleep. The TV was on, something about polar bears, but the sound had been turned down to a whisper.

"As you can see, she's just fine now. Poor little tyke had a rough night, though."

"Maddie, you're killing me with this suspense thing. Tell me what's happened, from the beginning."

Maddie Westfall said, "Perhaps we should have a nice cup of tea while we talk."

"No! I don't need tea. I'm an American, remember? All I need is to know what the heck is going on."

Still, Maddie seemed to take forever to adjust a light blanket she'd thrown over Amy. She fussed about, trying to determine how three people could sit in the two remaining chairs. Fiona solved that by sitting on the floor and leaning against the front of an overstuffed chair. Carter shrugged and sat behind with his legs straddling Fiona. He decided to stare at the back of Fiona's head and not say a word until Maddie decided to talk. *I'll sit here for a year, if that's what it takes.*

Maddie finally told her story. She still had no idea how she'd managed to miss Carter on his walk to the train station. When he told her about the footpath and the shortcut, she said, "How silly of me not to have anticipated that." Carter and Fiona both leaned forward when she got to the part about the neighbors calling the police.

"Ouch," said Fiona.

"So what happened after they left? I guess Mom's passed out in her bed."

"Oh, no. I mean, she may be asleep by now, but not in her bed. The police took her away."

It was Paddy O'Brien who ushered the two brothers into the warehouse. After they'd gone in, he stuck his head outside and looked toward the alley entrance. Then he slammed the door dramatically and leaned against it.

"What's going on?" said Fergie.

"Just waiting for Haverty is all," said O'Brien. Gordie wondered why he seemed so nervous.

Fergie took a few steps forward and looked around the room. "So where is he? I didn't think you had a key to this place."

"He went out to get some sweets and some root beer or something."

"He did *what*?"

"There's somebody comin' up the alley now, but I couldn't tell if it was him. Thought I'd best wait till we hear 'is knock."

"Sweets and root beer?"

"That's what he said."

"What the heck for?"

"Dunno. I didn't think it was my place to . . ."

There was a knock on the door, strong and authoritative.

"Guess it's 'im," said O'Brien. He opened the door a crack, and it crashed open, hitting him in the cheek. "Bloody 'ell."

"Bloody hell is right," said the figure in the doorway. Haverty stepped inside. "How stupid can you get? When you crack open a door, you put your foot against it solid, so no one can do what I just did. Idiot."

Fergie spoke up. "If it's the coppers putting a shoulder to the door, I don't think a foot's gonna stop 'em."

"It'll slow them down. Give us time to plan a counterattack."

"Yeah, sure."

"Anyway, there's little chance of them finding us. We've been right careful not to let nobody see us come in here. Right?"

Fergie shrugged.

"Right?"

"Of course right."

"I'm trusting you, Fergus. I know you ain't so stupid as O'Brien here, can't even put a foot against the door." O'Brien bristled and walked away, still rubbing the cheek that caught the full force of the blow.

Gordie said, "Do you really have sweets and root beer in that sack?"

"Couldn't find no root beer, but I got you some crème soda."

"I'm not really thirsty."

"It ain't for tonight. It's for tomorrow morning. You're gonna get yourselves down here before light. You'll for sure miss your breakfast, and lunch, too. Gotta have something to keep up your strength so's you don't get all weak from hunger, now don't we?"

"Tomorrow?"

"Oh, didn't I mention?" said Haverty. "We've stepped things up a bit. 'Stead of next week, we're gonna have our fireworks display tomorrow. I'm thinking you lads is gonna be onstage about 3:00 P.M., give or take. Just watch the telly, like we decided."

Gordie's heart was racing. He found it hard to breathe, yet he could feel his lungs pumping like crazy. It was going to happen. It was really going to happen. And he didn't have a week to get ready. Just a day. *Less* than a day, and he, Gordon Shamus McKenna, son of Durwin and Meara McKenna, not yet eighteen years old, was going to become a murderer.

Chapter 20

MADDIE WESTFALL NEEDED HELP FROM her friends. When she explained the situation to both C.C. and Babs, they insisted on coming to the Chamberlain house immediately. Maddie told them it would be fine to wait till morning, but they would have none of it. "In undertaking an intervention," said Babs, "it will be wise to plan ahead."

"Quite so," said C.C.

When Maddie hung up the phone, she told Carter, "Now, don't you worry, young man. I and my friends will have everything under control before you know it."

"But Maddie, what's an *intervention*?"

"It's something you do when someone you know, and especially someone you love, does things that are self-destructive. Like losing yourself to alcohol or drugs. You put yourself right in the middle of it, you *intervene*, and try to stop it."

"I've *been* trying. Trying and trying to stop her from drinking, but she won't listen."

"Of course not. She still thinks of you as a child. Adults don't take kindly to taking orders from children."

Fiona said, "Even if the child is right and the adult wrong?"

"Especially then. Think how it must be for her."

"The thing is, I can't much think of myself as a child anymore," said Carter. "Young maybe, but . . ."

"But it's not what *you* think, but how *she* feels, that's important here. I remember something my husband, Will, said to me before he died. He said, 'the only person over whom you have absolute control is yourself.' You can't *make* another person do something, and you can't *make* another person think something. All you can do is . . ."

"Is do or say something you *hope* will make them *want* to."

Maddie put her hand on Carter's shoulder. "Oh, Carter, those are almost exactly the same words my Will used. You really aren't a child anymore."

"Except to my mother."

"Well, yes. Like I say, like we are saying, there's no help for that. But I—I am older than your mother."

"And wiser."

Maddie smiled. "Now where have I heard that before?"

Fiona left, promising to phone Carter the next time her brothers went out on one of their furtive journeys. Carter helped Maddie bundle Amy into bed, and he collapsed on the couch. Maddie told him it was quite silly for him to stay up and wait for C.C. and Babs, as he'd had a long, hard day. She would wait for her friends, and they would plan their intervention. The police had no intention of releasing Carter's mother until morning, and until she was quite sober. No sense his not getting a good night's sleep.

When Carter woke up, he stumbled groggily toward the kitchen, thinking he might have time for a cup of coffee before Amy got up. The figure stretched out on the couch brought him up short, and the events of the night before came flooding back. He tried to creep as silently as possible so Maddie wouldn't wake up, but then he realized it wasn't Maddie. He wasn't sure whether it was the woman named C.C. or the one called Babs, but it definitely wasn't Maddie. The door to his parents' room was closed, so he decided to knock, loud enough for someone already awake to hear, but soft enough not to wake anyone. No one answered the knock, so he opened the door a crack and saw two figures on his parents' bed. Maddie and her friend. He shut the door, crept to the kitchen, and tried to make coffee without rattling anything. He was wearing a pair of yellow pajama bottoms and a black tee-shirt, what Amy called his bumblebee outfit. He figured he'd have time for a quick cup before he had to go change.

Carter was just settling down with coffee and a *National Geographic* when the phone rang. He jumped up to silence it before it woke up the houseful of women, but hit the edge of the table, spilling his coffee. Falling back, he tripped on his chair, which skittered across the kitchen and into the refrigerator. He added to the noise with a few choice words he was glad Amy wasn't there to hear.

It was Fiona on the phone, telling Carter her brothers had already sneaked out of the house. "They *never* go out in the morning. The pubs aren't open, so's they haven't any excuse, now, have they?"

"Where did they say they're going?"

"They wouldn't say at all. No reason. Just they got things to do. Gordie came and gave me a hug and said take good care of Mum. That scares me more than anything."

By now, Madeleine Westfall stood in the doorway, wrapped in a blanket. Carter sighed, rubbed his free hand over his face, and turned away from Maddie. In a quiet voice he said, "Fiona, I don't know what to do. Mom should be home some time this morning. I really need to . . ."

Maddie interrupted. "You need to help Fiona. You'll be worthless here. You're a child in this house, remember? But Fiona—Fiona needs a man right now. You can be assured my friends and I will do what is needed for your mother *and* your sister. Now go. But . . . before you do, you might want to put some clothes on."

Carter found Josh in his usual spot against the tile wall in Stepney Green Station. They shook hands. It seemed appropriate to be business-like for the business they were about.

"How'd you ditch the girl?" asked Josh.

"Fiona. Her name's Fiona. I didn't exactly ditch her. Just told her I couldn't get away till noon."

Josh looked at his watch. "It's, like, ten o'clock."

"Exactly. Maybe we can learn what we gotta learn, and I can be back in Northwood by then. She can't be mad at me if I have news about her brothers, can she?"

"I'm not a girl, *and* I'm not Irish. How the heck could I know if she'll be mad?"

"Well, I'll worry about that when the time comes. I don't have the power to make her feel any particular way. I can only do things I think might make her *want* to feel the way I want her to feel."

"Carter, have you been smokin' something?"

Carter didn't answer. He was already on his way up the escalator, with Josh trying to keep up. Outside, Carter slowed and motioned for his companion to take the lead. "Your show, Watson. Lead on, my good man. Lead on."

Josh started down the street and stopped at the second intersection. "I'm pretty sure they turned left here."

"You're pretty sure?"

"Well, it was dark then, you know. It all looks different in the daytime."

"I don't think Sherlock's sidekick would have . . ."

"If we come to Brixton Road, I'll know where we are. Find the bakery shop I told you about with an alley next door. That's the alley."

They found Brixton Road, the bakery, and the alley. "Now," said Josh, "we just need to find the building."

"757."

"You have an excellent memory, Sherlock."

"If you want something remembered well, remember it yourself. I think I heard that somewhere."

"You're full of witty sayings this morning. Now what do you say we do? There's number 757 up ahead. Do we barge in, knock and say 'pizza delivery,' or what?"

"Good question. From what I remember about Sherlock Holmes, he spent his time quietly deducing things. I don't remember him having to be active. Take risks and stuff. Come to think of it, that's what he had Watson do for him while he sat in an easy chair and smoked his crooked pipe."

"And yet, here you are."

"Decidedly so, my man. Here I am indeed."

"So, Sherlock, will it be pizza or Chinese?"

"Maybe we can be from the electric company, here to check the meters."

"Will Fergus or Gordon recognize you? You've been hanging with their sister, after all."

"I've never been to Fiona's house, and that time I bumped into them on the train, they had no idea."

"I have an idea now, mates." Carter and Josh spun toward the voice behind them.

"Jeez."

"How did? . . ."

"I had me eye on you two blokes since I turned the corner. Kinda got me curiosity raised, your standin' all this time in front of this particular door. So I come up quiet-like, and sure enough, you're so busy figuring out what to do next, you didn't even look around."

Carter cursed under his breath. *Stupid. Stupid. Stupid. How stupid can we get?*

By Carter's reckoning, the man was in his mid-thirties. He was wearing black trousers and a navy blue windbreaker. On his head was a black-and-brown cloth cap. He had his hands on his hips, and he was lowering and raising his face, like he was studying Carter and Josh from head to toe. Finally, he said, "Well, since you want so bad to go through that door, let me help." He reached between them and rapped twice.

After a few seconds, the door opened a crack.

"You can take your foot off the door now, O'Brien. It's Haverty."

The door opened wider, and a face peered from around the side. The man called Haverty said, "Ah, it's you, Fergie. Open it full now, would ye?" He stepped back, grabbed Josh and Carter by the shoulders, and thrust them through the doorway.

Josh cried out when he hit the side of the door. Carter choked back his own cry and clenched his fists so he couldn't rub the side of an arm throbbing in pain from his own collision with the woodwork. He wasn't going to give this Haverty the satisfaction.

Besides Haverty and Fergus McKenna, two others were in the room. Carter recognized Fiona's twin brother Gordon, who had jumped up from where he sat on the floor in front of a television set. The other one was probably O'Brien.

"Who the heck are these guys?" said Fergie.

"I don't, to be perfectly honest, ken who they are," said Haverty, "but these two blokes seem to know you and Gordie here."

"Don't see how."

"Well, outside the door, they was discussin' your sister. Seems like they know her."

Gordie had hung back through this conversation, standing with his hands clasped together in front of the flickering TV screen. Now he rushed forward with his hands outstretched. Palms up. "How do you know Fiona? Who the hell are you?"

Carter had to step back to avoid Gordie's charge. Carter's mind was racing. *Who are we supposed to be under these circumstances?* He was cursing himself again. They'd been dim-witted and careless, not seeing Haverty approach outside. Now, he realized, they had no plan, no plan at all, for this situation. *Stupid. Stupid. Stupid.*

Josh blurted out, "Don't know what you're talking about. We weren't talking about anyone's sister. Whose sister?"

Carter groaned inwardly. This Haverty had clearly heard them outside. Lying about it would just make it worse. *Make us look guilty. But . . . what could we possibly say that would make us look not* guilty?

He decided the truth, or something close to the truth, would have to do. "Fiona was worried about you two. She asked me to make sure you weren't in any kind of trouble." He looked from Fergie to Gordie and added, "She loves you, ya know."

It was Gordie's turn to step back. He held his hands to his sides and lowered his chin to his chest. Haverty slugged his shoulder and said, "Back to the telly, Gordon. Fergie, take control of your little brother. Paddy and I'll handle this now." He grabbed Josh, spun him around, pushed him down, and kicked out his feet in what seemed to Carter a really professional move. He put a foot onto Josh's back.

"There's rope in the bag over there, Paddy. Tie this bugger's hands."

Carter froze. He wanted to fight, wanted to help Josh, wanted to run for the door, wanted to be somewhere else, wanted . . .

The door won. He made a dash for it, reasoning he couldn't help Josh with three against one. He had to find help somewhere. But it was too late. He was fumbling with the latch when he was caught on the side of the head by something that felt like lead. Bright lights flashed in his brain, and he spun to the side. For a brief instant he had a vision of Fergus McKenna holding a piece of pipe over his head as he slumped to the ground. The sight of Fergie, the flashing lights, all faded away into darkness.

Maddie and Babs rummaged through the kitchen, looking for something to make a decent breakfast, while C.C. stripped the bed and put the sheets into the washer. "We want everything to be all fresh and nice for Mrs. Chamberlain," Maddie had said. "Now, don't we?"

The search for breakfast foods was coming up empty. There were two boxes of dry cereal, both with a few flakes rattling in the bottom, no milk, no eggs. Babs said, "I believe one of us should go pick up some food, don't you think?"

"That would be quite appropriate, I believe," said Maddie. "The little tyke, Amy, will be starved, I believe. She had a very trying time yesterday. Eggs would be nice, and milk, and stop by the butcher's for some bangers or perhaps a lovely rasher of bacon. The thick kind, mind you. The girl needs her energy."

"I think it's *your* energy you're concerned with, my dear."

When Amy wandered out of her bedroom, bleary-eyed and yawning, Maddie hugged her and told her everything would be fine, just fine. Amy seemed confused, as if she couldn't really remember the events of the previous day. *Just as well,* thought Maddie. *Just as well.*

"My good friend Babs, Mrs. Kroome, has gone to get us some lovely food so we can have a lovely breakfast. Isn't that nice?" Amy nodded, tentatively. "She'll be back shortly. In the meantime, why don't you go get dressed, dear? You'll feel ever so much better." Amy shrugged, signaling she wasn't sure how getting dressed would make her feel better. Maddie Westfall decided to maintain a cheery disposition, *for the little tyke's sake.* "Now, Amy, would you like for me to pick out some clothes and help you dress? Or are you a big girl now and don't need help?"

Amy stood for a moment with her mouth open, before she croaked out a single word, "Big."

When Babs got back, she and Maddie bustled about the kitchen, cooking and setting the table. There was a small bouquet of marigolds on the table, now wilted and dropping petals to the Formica. Maddie thought it was a depressing sign that someone had tried to bring a note of cheer into this unhappy house. *Now look at it. Poor thing, falling apart like the family that lives here.*

They were in the middle of breakfast: eggs over easy, toast with marmalade, and bacon, the thick kind, when the phone rang. It was the police, saying they were ready to release Mrs. Chamberlain. Was there anyone who could come to the station and pick her up?

"Oh, dear. I'm quite afraid no one here has an automobile, young man. We use our feet and legs for all of our . . ."

"All right, madam. We shall bring her home. You will be there, won't you?"

"Of course. My friends and I are here to do whatever needs done to help the poor lady and her poor daughter."

"Okay. Need to warn you, though. She's sober now, but I'm afraid to say she was an awful lot easier to handle when she was drunk. This woman is . . . well, good luck to you."

Maddie hung up the phone and told Amy her mum was on her way home, "and we need to all be helpful and pleasant." To C.C. and Babs she added, smiling for Amy's benefit, "Of course, girls, an intervention may not be pleasurable, but we shall try. We shall certainly try."

Carter's first sensation was the hardness of the floor he was lying on. He was flat on his stomach. His entire chest and the bone at the base of his stomach were aching from the pressure of his body. Next, he was aware of a dirty concrete floor stretching out to where it disappeared under a table or a bench. It was dark under the table, but the floor in front could be seen covered in splotches of paint and bits of trash. He tried to lift his head, but whenever he did, a sharp pain drove it back down. It was a little easier to turn to the side. Still painful, but the ache subsided once he quit moving. To the side he could see the backs of two people and beyond them the bluish light of a television screen. The two were watching the screen intently, not moving at all.

Carter decided he would endure the pain and push himself up into a sitting position so he could decide what to do next. He remembered Josh, prone on the floor with a foot in his back, and wondered where his friend was now. When he tried to bring his hands forward, he found they wouldn't move! He became aware of an ache in his wrists that matched the pains underneath. His wrists were tied behind his back, and no amount of struggling could get them loose.

He had to lift his head off the floor in order to turn it the other direction. As he hoped, sure enough, there was Josh lying parallel to him. He was on his side, holding his arms in a way that showed his hands were tied, too. Josh was staring at Carter and smiling weakly. "Good morning, Carter. Have a nice nap?"

"Screw you, Josh. I'm dying here."

"For a while I thought you might be. But now you're able to cuss out your buddy, I can see you're all right."

"If you think being all right's having a headache so bad all the other aches seem like . . . well, not so bad."

Carter could see a pair of legs that had come over to stand between them. He tried to tilt his head up enough to see who it was, but quit trying when he heard Fergie's voice. "So you decided to join us, huh, fella? What is it your chum here called you? Carter? Sounds a posh kinda name for a fella lying on a dirty floor."

"I wouldn't be on the floor if it wasn't for . . ."

"Sorry about that, old boy. I did have to keep you from, shall we say, leaving the premises. I never coshed a bloke with a piece a pipe before, but it worked good, didn't it?"

"A threat would have worked fine, too. You didn't have to actually use it."

"Figured I needed the practice. In a couple hours, might need to use it for real."

"What happens in a couple of hours?"

"Let's just say Gordie and Paddy and I are gonna go make history. Ain't that right, boys?"

Someone Carter assumed was Paddy O'Brien said, "Damn right, Fergie, old chum. Those blighters at Burlington Arcade won't know what hit 'em."

"We shouldn't be telling where we're going." The voice was Fergie's brother Gordon.

"What difference does it make?" This time it was Fergie. "Haverty said not to worry none about that kinda thing. He'd clean up all the pieces later, when we're done."

Carter's heart sank. If Haverty didn't care if his prisoners knew what was going down, it could only mean one thing. *Haverty has no intention of letting us out of this alive.*

It seemed like hours, but was probably only minutes, when he heard Fergie shout, "It's happening, lads. Time to get ready." He had rushed to join the other two sitting in front of the television. They were all on their knees, now, cheering like they were watching a soccer match. Carter couldn't see the picture, but he could hear what sounded like an excited announcer. The sound was too low for him to catch all the words, but snatches came through. "Horseguards . . . the Queen's own men . . . Hyde Park . . . dreadful explosion . . . oh, the horror of it . . . all those gallant men, those beautiful, beautiful horses . . ."

O'Brien was shouting, "This is it. This is it. One more and we go. One more and we go."

Carter saw one of the three figures quietly get up and walk between him and Josh to the far wall. He managed to turn his head enough to follow him to a corner of the room, where he stood, facing the wall. His shoulders were shaking violently. *He's crying. One of them is crying.*

"Get your butt outta the corner, Gordie." It was Fergie calling out. "This is what we been waiting for. The big show is under way, kiddo."

Gordie said, between sobs, "I never thought. Never thought he'd blow up horses. Guys riding their horses in a parade."

"These is the *Queen's* Horseguards, man. These ain't just any soldiers. He's gotten to the blokes what parade around for Her Bloody Majesty herself."

"I know. But I keep thinking about what happens if our sister ever learns what we're up to. I been telling myself we can explain the need for it, you know, to sacrifice a few people to save a lot of them. But with these horses, there's no way she'll ever come to forgive us."

Carter tried to speak, even though the pain only allowed short gasps. "Gordie's right . . . she wants to . . . heal horses . . . you want . . . kill."

"Shut yer gob, American boy," said Fergie. "You got nothin' to say here."

Paddy O'Brien said from across the room, "Don't matter much what he says, or what he hears, for that matter. Haverty said he'd clean things up here when he got back."

Carter groaned inwardly. He and O'Brien shared one thing. Both had the same understanding of what Haverty meant by "clean up."

Fiona McKenna busied herself about the house, cleaning the kitchen, feeding Kerry Girl, helping Mum sit up in front of her bedroom telly with tea and scones and the last dollop of strawberry jam in the jar. She glared at the clock—still two hours till noon. *Maybe Carter can come a wee bit earlier.* She decided to give him a call. *All he can say is no.*

The telephone was answered by an unfamiliar woman's voice.

"Maddie?"

"Oh, no, dear, this is Maddie's friend C.C. Can I tell her who's on the line?"

"This is Fiona. Did I meet you at? . . ."

"Of course, dear. We had a lovely chat. Maddie's gone to the loo, I'm afraid, but I shall have her call you the minute she's back."

"No, that's all right. It's Carter I want to talk to."

"Oh, my. Carter left the house some time ago. Two hours—maybe more. He wanted to stay, for when his mum gets home, but Maddie insisted he go."

"Go to . . ."

"I'm not certain. I overheard him say something to Maddie about London, but of course London is a very large place. I know I'm not being very helpful, my dear."

Fiona was stunned. When she finally spoke, it was barely above a whisper. "That's quite all right. I know where he's gone, and why. Tell Maddie . . ."

"Tell her what, dear?"

"Nothing. Just tell her I called."

Fiona sat staring at the tabletop for a moment, then leaped to her feet. She'd never catch up with Carter and his friend, but she had to—absolutely *had* to—get herself to Stepney Green, and quickly. How dare he lie to her, treat her like a child? How dare he run off by himself after promising to take her with him? *To keep poor little me out of trouble. He's as much a male chauvinist as all the others.*

She was gathering up her jacket and purse before she had another thought. *What if I go running off to London at the same time Carter's coming back here? Two trains passing in a tunnel.* She decided to go on with her busywork around the house until he contacted her. It was almost lunch, so she prepared a bite for herself and took a tray up to her mother. Mum was still watching the telly. Fiona could never tell whether she was actually processing the programs in her mind, or just being mesmerized by flickering lights and sounds. She never reacted in any way, no matter what was on. News programs, dramas, children's cartoons—it didn't seem to matter.

After lunch, Fiona settled into an easy chair with Kerry Girl on her lap. She started to read a magazine she'd just brought home, the latest *Horse and Hound*, when she heard a strangled cry from upstairs. It rose in volume to a scream, then subsided.

Kerry Girl went flying, barking in alarm. By the time Fiona reached the upstairs hallway and then the bedroom door, her mother was moaning, the sound rhythmically pulsing as she rocked back and forth against the headboard.

"Mum, what is it? What's the matter?" Fiona rushed to insert a hand behind her mother's head, hoping the banging hadn't already caused some damage.

Her mother pointed to the television screen, where a mike-holding reporter was talking in front of a milling crowd of people. Fiona rushed to the set and turned it off, then went back to her mother and took hold of a trembling hand.

"Mum, what is it? It's been ages since you . . . oh, Mum. You're back. You're back. But why are you so frightened? What's happened?"

Fiona's mother pointed again at the now-dark TV screen and said, in a voice cracking with emotion, "Men with guns. Explosions. Oh, Fiona, your father is dead. They shot him. He's dead." She reached out and cupped her hand against Fiona's face. "Oh, my poor girl. What will we do now?"

Fiona couldn't believe what she was hearing. Her mother was back, but it was like time had stopped six years ago. She seemed to think Pa had just been killed. Didn't she know it was 1982, that they'd allowed Uncle Corey to uproot them from their Belfast home and bring them here to this foreign place? Didn't she know Uncle Corey had finally abandoned his whole family, disappearing to who-knows-where, leaving a wife and children in Ireland and his sick sister-in-law and three kids in England, all of them getting by on handouts from the government?

"Look at me, Mum. Do I look eleven years old? I'm seventeen, Mum. Seventeen."

Her mother shook her head and looked down at her lap. When she looked up, she gave Fiona a tightlipped smile and said, "I know, Fiona. I know time has passed, it's just I don't remember it. All I see is a bit here, a bit there, and I know time has gone by, but I don't remember any of it." She shook her head. "Just a little at a time, pieces, like in a dream."

"Oh, Mum, I'm so glad to have you back." She had another thought. "You will stay, won't you?"

"I . . . I hope so, Fiona. I hope so. I saw something on the telly that frightened me something awful. I could almost hear the gunshots that killed your Pa. It was . . . where are your brothers? I need to see them."

Fiona stammered, "They . . . they're out. London, I think."

"London? London, England?"

"Yes, Mum. We live in a place called Northwood. It's about a half-hour's train ride from London, England."

Fiona's mother was crying now. "I just don't understand. How did we get here? Where are my boys? Fiona, I need my children here. All of them."

Two of Meara McKenna's children were, at that moment, scurrying around an old warehouse, packing blasting caps, an electrical switch, and wiring into a cardboard box that already held twenty sticks of dynamite. They packed some scraps of lumber and paper into two identical boxes. Haverty had said it didn't make sense for the three of them to go into Burlington Arcade carrying a single box. "That'd be stupid now, wouldn't it? And none a you lot is stupid, right?" They'd all nodded, though Carter suspected not a one of them would have thought about bringing two dummy boxes.

Carter's head was feeling better now, but the hard floor was pressing into him worse every minute, and he was getting a tingly feeling in his hands. He'd heard of people whose hands had frozen, and they'd gotten gangrene because the blood couldn't flow through them. Would the same thing happen if his were tied? He hated the idea of losing his hands, then thought, *What does it matter? I'm probably not going to be alive to miss them. I'd miss Amy and Mom and . . . I suppose I mean they'd miss me.*

He thought about his dad, somewhere in Europe eating fancy food with his secretary, not knowing his son was tied up like a goat about to be slaughtered. Didn't even know his wife had managed to get herself thrown in jail. Didn't know his youngest daughter had been so terrified, it took an old lady's kindness to calm her down.

He needed to talk one of his captors into loosening his hands or at least letting him sit up. The older brother, Fergie, would never do it. He was too eaten up by something—hatred?—or sorrow? Hard to tell, but he was very deliberately going about the job of assembling a bomb to blow people up. O'Brien was even worse. He was almost bubbling over with enthusiasm at the thought of killing people. Carter shuddered.

Only the younger brother, Gordie they called him, seemed like his heart wasn't fully into their deadly plans. Carter had seen him trying to hide the fact he was crying. Besides, hadn't Fiona told him Gordie was her twin brother? Aren't twins supposed to take after each other? Fiona is sweet and loves all creatures, human and otherwise. Shouldn't Gordie be the same? *Then what the heck is he doing here?*

As soon as he saw Gordie near where he and Josh were lying, and the other two were across the room, he called out, "Gordie. Psst. Hey, Gordie."

Gordie stood above Carter, who had to twist his head almost backward to see him. "I can't talk to you," said Gordie.

"You don't need to talk. Just help me get more comfortable. This hard floor is killing me."

Gordie squatted down and whispered to Carter, "This floor is all we got."

"There's a workbench over there. Help me sit up and lean against it. You can tie me to the leg. I'll be even more tied up than now."

After several more pleas and refusals, Gordie said, "I gotta get more rope." A minute later he was back and helped Carter half roll, half crawl to the bench. He helped lift him up against a bench leg. Before he could use the new rope to tie Carter in place, someone from across the room shouted, "What the heck you doin'? Gordie, you nitwit. Put him back."

"I just thought it'd be safer to have him tied up to this table leg, so's he can't run away."

"The door's locked, and his hands is tied behind his back. Where's he gonna run?"

"I just thought . . ."

"You ain't paid to think, little brother. Just do."

"So what do I do now, big brother? Haul him back to the middle of the floor and sit on him?"

"No. I guess you've done it, so ya might as soon tie him there."

Gordie hooked a piece of fresh rope to the one lashed between Carter's hands and then tied it to the bench leg. "There, that should be good."

"Good enough," said Fergie. "Oh, heck. Help me haul the other fellow over here, too. Might as well tidy up the place." They worked together to drag Josh to another table leg and hoist him into position. Gordie tied his hands to the post. He and Fergie stood back to survey what they'd done. "Guess it ain't such a bad thing," said Fergie. "Given as it come from my blockhead of a brother. One more thing we got to do is stuff a rag in their mouths so they don't wake the neighbors when we leave 'em." He rummaged around on one of the workbenches and found two rags. He wrapped one around a short piece of rope and placed it on Carter's face. "Be a good lad and open up now. It's gotta be in your mouth, or it don't do no good."

"It smells like motor oil."

"If you don't put that thing in your mouth, you won't be smelling nothing."

When both Carter and Josh were gagged and gagging from the stench of grease, Fergie nodded in satisfaction and walked away. Gordie followed, but turned back briefly, to nod at Carter. His face was solemn, but Carter was sure he saw a small note of sympathy in the younger McKenna's eyes. Maybe what they say about twins wasn't so far off the mark.

Chapter 21

FIONA HAD AN ALMOST INSOLUBLE PROBLEM. How could she leave her mother now that Mum had miraculously regained her senses? Now, instead of lying inertly in her bed or an easy chair, oblivious to everything around, Meara McKenna was awake and feeling things. And what she was feeling was terror. Terror at waking in a strange place with six years of life missing. Terror at reliving the death of her husband, whose murder seemed to her like yesterday, a fresh wound still tearing at her heart. *Mum needs her family here, her whole family.* Her brothers had run off to London, and Carter had followed them. Hours and hours ago. Why hadn't she heard from him? If he was going to be delayed, he could have called. *He has to know I'd be frightened when noon came and went. Oh, Carter, what am I going to do?*

She decided to see if Maddie had an idea. She called the Chamberlain home and was relieved to hear a familiar voice. "Maddie? It's Fiona. I guess I need your help one more time."

After hearing Fiona's story, Maddie said, "My dear girl, I would come to your house immediately, but we're expecting Carter's mother home at any moment. Still, here is the good news. My girlfriends Babs and C.C. are with me. Since our help is required in two places, it would seem we must organize into teams. Now, let's see . . . I'm quite sure Mrs. Chamberlain will be the more difficult charge, so two of us will stay here. Babs and me, I think. C.C. will proceed to your house to assist with your mother."

"But all I wanted was your advice."

"So, I advise you to fix a nice cup of tea for your mum and yourself, and have one ready for C.C. when she gets there. I'm certain Carter has your address here somewhere, my dear, but finding it would be more difficult than locating a pen to write it down again."

C.C. Piper had no sooner left for her short journey to Northwood when there was a knock on the door. Two disgruntled-looking police officers stood on the porch. Between them was a woman with an even more sour expression on her face. She opened her mouth at the sight of Madeleine Westfall, and finally blurted out, "Who the hell are you?"

The encounter didn't get much better when they'd retreated into the living room. The two cops looked liked their minds were divided between staying to prevent a hair-pulling female wrestling match and a desire to escape just as fast as their legs would take them. Maddie solved their dilemma by shooing them out the door, saying, "Be gone with you now. We ladies have this well in hand."

"You sure?"

"Are you calling me an addle-brained female? You men are all alike. Of course I'm sure."

Nelda Chamberlain collapsed sullenly into a chair, the same easy chair her son had sat in the night before. Maddie stood in front of her for a minute, then started for the kitchen. "You talk to Babs here, won't you, my dear? I think this calls for a spot of tea."

Babs tried to start a conversation twice, but both times Nelda turned her face away abruptly. She clearly had no wish to talk to this strange woman who had come uninvited into her home. Maddie sized up the situation the minute she returned with a tray of tea, cups, saucers, milk, and sugar. She wanted to inject some cheer into the situation, but decided that would probably backfire. *I'd best be as quiet as the others. Let Mrs. Chamberlain be the one to break the silence.* She set a cup of tea down on a side table, and when Nelda glanced her way, she gestured with the milk and sugar service. Nelda stared for a moment, then shook her head. Another moment and she reached for her teacup. *Yes,* thought Maddie. *We are making progress.*

When Nelda Chamberlain finally spoke, it was barely above a whisper. "Just what is it you're doing here? And who . . . who are you, anyway?"

Babs looked at Maddie, who said, "I'm just an old lady who met your son Carter a few weeks ago. In that time, I've come to care for the boy, for the young man, quite a lot. I think it fair to say I am his friend. And Babs here is *my* friend."

"You still have no right to come into my house, make yourself at home. Make my tea."

"You are absolutely correct, my dear. Even though we were invited by your son, I do recognize this is *your* home. It's just that . . . Amy needed looking after, and you were . . . somewhat indisposed for a bit."

Nelda shook her head. "You're not making sense. If Amy needed help, it's Carter's job to help her, not two . . . two strange women. Where is he, anyway? What have you done with Carter?"

"It's complicated. But you're not to worry. Carter is one of the most level-headed young men I've ever met. I am absolutely sure he has taken care of whatever business he was about and will walk in that door any minute now."

Fiona called the Chamberlain residence one more time, in hopes Carter had gone straight home. Maddie Westfall answered the phone and told her Carter still hadn't returned, and no, he hadn't called. His mother was home now, bless her, but she'd fallen asleep on the couch. "Shall I have Carter phone you when he arrives?"

"Yes . . . no, I'm going out. I'll ring him up when I get back."

Fiona had made up her mind. Carter and the brothers had been gone far too long. She was going to Stepney Green to find them. Or try. If they passed in the subway tunnels like ships in the night, so be it. Somehow she had to drag Fergie and Gordie away from whatever it was they were doing. *They surely won't be angry when they find out about Mum.*

She had to wait for the arrival of C.C. Piper, of course. When the older woman walked in the door, she was all "My dearie" and "Tut, tut, not to worry" and "Fiddlesticks, it's no bother." She had the same cheery, take-charge disposition as Maddie. She didn't even wait for Fiona to introduce her to her mum, but took over the conversation immediately. "I'm Crista Cordelia Piper, but everyone calls me C.C. I hope you will, too, my dear. I've become great friends with your daughter. Lovely girl, you've done a marvelous job with her. I'm told your two boys are among the missing today, but not to worry. Fiona will have them back in a flash. Now, you sit right there and enjoy your telly while I toddle off to the kitchen. Fiona, dearie, would you be so kind as to show me where I can find the tea-making supplies? Then you can be away to find your brothers." Fiona was out of breath just listening to her.

Stepney Green Station was almost deserted. In this part of London, there wasn't much lunch hour traffic, and what there was had tapered off. On the streets, she tried to remember what Josh had said about the building her brothers had disappeared into. It was down an alley, and the alley was off Brixton Road next to some kind of shop. *Greengrocers? Butchers? Some kind of food store, for sure.* When she got to Brixton Road, she found there were all kinds of food stores. It seemed hopeless until she realized none of the ones in sight was at the corner of an alley. Then she saw it. "Ghardello's Pastries." And right beyond it was the opening to an alley.

The next problem was finding the building. Josh had mentioned a number, and Carter had undoubtedly stored it away in his memory, but her brain wasn't wired that way. She could scarcely remember her own telephone number. She walked the length of the alley, hoping for some bit of inspiration, but none came. At the far end, she leaned against a dilapidated red telephone kiosk, trying to figure out her next move. Just then, a small moving lorry rumbled down the street behind her and swerved into the alley. She had to jump back to prevent it running over her foot. She took a few steps toward the retreating van and shook her fist, prepared to let loose with a few choice Irish cuss-words. Then she decided they would be wasted on the dust that kicked up behind the vehicle, even though it had slowed way down to avoid an alley littered with potholes. It stopped about halfway through the alley, and the driver opened the rear doors. He knocked on the side of the building, after looking furtively both ways. She heard him holler "O'Brien," the door opened, then a minute later, he and a pair of men came out carrying three large boxes, which they loaded carefully into the van. They shut the doors and leaped into the front seat with the driver. They moved off, slowly at first, then faster.

By this time, Fiona was shouting and running as fast as she could. As soon as the two men had deposited their loads in the back of the van and turned sideways to jump into the front seat, she had seen their profiles and recognized Fergie and Gordie. She hadn't gone twenty feet when she stumbled in a pothole and fell face forward. She managed to prevent her nose from hitting the pavement, but the pain in her hands was excruciating. She pulled herself into a sitting position and watched her brothers disappear around the corner on Brixton Road, then assessed the damage to her palms. They were scratched and bleeding lightly, but nothing seemed broken. Her skirt was torn, too, but she'd worry about that later. At the moment, she needed to see if she could find out where her brothers had gone. *Maybe the answer is somewhere in that building they just left. And another thing. Where the heck is Carter?*

Fiona wasn't quite sure from which door her brothers had come. From a distance, you couldn't really tell. Then she saw one labeled with weatherbeaten lettering that read "757." *This must be it. I remember thinking the number sounded like some kind of airplane.* She tried the door handle, but it wouldn't turn. She beat on the door with her fists, calling out, "Is anyone in there? Can you hear me? Anybody there?" Completely frustrated, she pounded harder, yelling frantically until she could barely choke out another cry. She leaned her head on the door and let the tears flow. And then . . . and then she realized the door had responded to her pounding and moved. Not more than a fraction of an inch, but it had moved! Her hands were throbbing in pain, so she put her shoulder to the door and shoved as hard as she could. *Yes. Fergie and Gordie had been carrying those heavy boxes. Wizard, they didn't stop to see the door was latched.* Slowly, Fiona managed to shove the heavy door open, revealing a shadowy room, brightened only by the flickering light of a television screen. As far as she could tell, the telly was playing to an empty room.

From his new vantage point, propped up against the leg of the workbench, Carter had been able to watch the three bombmakers assembling their lethal apparatus on another bench across the room. They had turned the television screen so they could watch it while they worked. From where he was tied, Carter couldn't see the screen, and the sound was too low to carry well across the warehouse floor. From the renewed excitement in the announcer's voice and the whoops and hollers of the bombers, he assumed a second explosion had occurred somewhere, and this was the signal for his captors to go and do their own dirty work. This was borne out when Fergie started reading out items from a list, and the other two searched through one of the boxes and called out, "Check."

Before they finished with this routine, the one called O'Brien said, "I'd best be off and bring the lorry around. You lot finish the checkoff and be ready to roll when I gets back." He left in a hurry, allowing the door to creak shut behind him. A few seconds later, he pushed it back open a crack and shouted, "And don't ye forget nothin'." Then he banged the door closed, rattled the knob, and left.

About ten minutes later, there was a pounding at the door, and Fergie called out to make sure it was O'Brien. It was, so they flung the door open, propped it with a brick, and each grabbed the boxes from the work table. "I'll take the bomb," said Fergie. "You two take the dummies."

"I suppose you think that's fitting, don't you?" said Gordie.

"You said it, little brother, not me. But now you know . . ."

O'Brien carried his box out the door first, then Gordie. Fergie followed with his, stopping to click off the light and kick the brick away so the door would close behind him.

When they were gone, Carter thought about the predicament he and Josh were in. They were tied up with their hands tight in back. Carter's arms and shoulders had stopped hurting, and they were now as numb as his fingers. His head still hurt when he shook it, but it wasn't too bad. *Just don't shake it, you idiot.* He had tried to wiggle his hands to loosen the ropes, but they were on too tight. *Probably why I'm getting numb.* He wondered if he could somehow push up under the workbench and lift it, then he could slip the ropes out under the legs. It was probably way too heavy, and there was no way he could get his own legs under him to even try it. That seemed like a dead end.

He had abandoned all hope of coming up with a solution, and his thoughts turned to his family. With him gone, who would take care of Amy? Would there be anyone who could, or would, help his mother find her way out of the dark place she was in? Wrapped in these dismal thoughts, he heard a pounding at the door and the muffled sound of someone shouting. He tried to shout back but only managed a pitiful "aargh" through the gag. Carter wondered why Josh was silent, and assumed he knew it was useless to communicate with someone whose own voice could barely be heard through the heavy door.

Amazingly, a small sliver of light appeared in the darkness where the door was located. Carter held his breath, wondering what was happening. The crack of light held steady for a moment then began to widen. *Yes! Someone's coming in.* Then Carter had a sudden thought. Since the person coming through that door had a key, then it could be one of the bombers, or someone working with them. He looked over at Josh and thought he could see his face shaking back and forth. *That's why he's keeping quiet. He already figured it might be one of the bad guys.* Carter turned his attention back to the door. It was now mostly open, and he could see the silhouette of a figure slip through and disappear again in the gloom. The brief look gave him the impression the person was slim and a bit shorter than any of the bombers. Whoever it was had stopped shouting before the door started to open, and he was definitely quiet now, standing just inside the doorway and not even moving.

When the mysterious stranger started to move again, it was back toward the door. Carter's mind was racing. *If he leaves, we'll never know if he's friend or foe. But if I cry out, I might be sorry.* It was crunch time, and he had to make a decision. Then he realized the shadowy figure had gone near the door but wasn't going out. Instead he was moving sideways, slowly. Carter guessed what was happening. The person was searching along the wall for a light switch. *If he finds one, it won't make much difference whether I make noise, will it? Josh and me, we'll be like a couple of caged animals at the zoo, or a . . .*

The light, striking six eyes used to the dark, was blinding.

When he could finally focus on the mystery figure by the front wall of the warehouse, Carter nearly choked trying to cry out through the oily rag in his mouth. It was Fiona. Couldn't be, but it was. He could see Fiona swiveling her head, trying to locate the source of the garbled noise. Her eyes found Josh, then Carter, and she screamed. She seemed frozen for several seconds before she ran to Carter and threw herself down in front of him. She screamed again when her hands hit the warehouse floor, and she pulled herself, painfully it seemed, into a kneeling position, and clenched her hands together in front of her chin. Carter could see streaks of blood oozing out between her fingers.

"Oh, Carter. How did you? . . . I knew something was wrong. I just knew it."

Carter twisted his mouth trying unsuccessfully to move the gag. Fiona said, "Keep still, I'll try to get it out." She waddled beside him on her knees and reached behind to work on the knots tying the gag in place. She cried in frustration, "No. No. It's too tight and my hands . . . I can't do it. Gotta find something." She slowly pulled herself standing and then rushed from workbench to workbench, searching for something to cut the cords binding Carter and his friend. When she came back, she was holding a screwdriver.

"I couldn't find any kind of knife, but I brought this. Maybe I can stick it through the knot and get it to loosen up. That's what I do when I tangle up me tatting yarn." Sure enough, after she struggled with it for some time, she said, "It's coming. Just a little more." In another minute, Carter could feel the gag loosening, and then it was out. He opened his mouth and breathed in great gulps of air.

Fiona was talking. ". . . and get you loose from the table leg. Hold still."

"I'm not going anywhere."

"Oh, that was silly of me. 'Course you're not. What I meant was . . ."

"I know what you meant," said Carter. "It just feels so good to say something to get my mind off . . . well, you know."

It took longer to get the knot holding Carter to the bench leg undone, but when it was, he carefully brought his hands in front of himself and studied them while he flexed his shoulder muscles. Some of him ached like crazy, while part of him was totally numb.

Fiona said, "Do you want to untie your friend?"

Carter shook his head. "I can't feel anything in my hands. Yet. You did a good job on me, so can you do Josh, too? By the way, what's wrong with *your* hands?"

"I'll tell you all about it later. They're fine."

Josh had been watching this procedure patiently, it seemed to Carter, who thought, *Damn. I should have had her take out his gag before she untied me from the table leg.* Aloud, he said, "Josh, you look like something roasting on a spit at a Hawaiian luau."

The second it was out of his mouth, he wanted to pull it back. Not that Josh didn't need some cheering up, but it suddenly hit him this was no time for humor. The two of them had knowledge of something horrible that was going to happen soon, something that was maybe going to kill a lot of people. And the truth of the matter was, it was up to Josh Weaver and Carter Chamberlain to try to stop it. *Yeah, right. The bombers have a half-hour lead on us. Fat chance.*

As Josh was flexing his muscles and trying to suck in some fresh air to clear his lungs, Fiona wandered over to the television set where the announcer's excitement was apparent even to Carter at the far side of the huge room. Fiona could be seen to gasp and then cry out, and Carter hurried to her as quickly as his almost-paralyzed legs could move him. She grabbed his arm when he came near.

"It's horrible. Mum watched something awful on the telly earlier, but I turned it off before I saw what it was. This is . . . I've never seen the likes of this. He's saying a lot of soldiers have been blown up. They were a band playing music somewhere. Regents Park or Hyde Park, I think. And some others were riding horses. Carter, I can't stand this. They say horses were blown up, too." Fiona clung tighter to Carter and pressed her head against his shoulder. He could feel her shaking.

Carter had never felt lower than he did at that moment. What he was watching on television was bad enough, but what he had to say was worse. He was going to have to tell this sobbing girl, who was holding onto him for comfort, that her two brothers were a part of the horror she was watching. Worse, they were on their way to someplace called Burlington Arcade loaded with a bomb, a bomb that would be used to kill even more innocent people.

Chapter 22

FIONA TOOK THE NEWS ABOUT HER BROTHERS better than Carter feared. She gasped, but got totally quiet and walked to a corner of the room and stood, facing a blank wall. Then he realized it wasn't better at all. When she'd screamed and clung to him, it was at least possible for him to share the grief and give her whatever comfort he could. But now... now, she had taken herself off alone, and she'd sealed her feelings up inside, with him on the outside. Carter felt totally helpless. He looked at Josh, who shrugged.

Josh said, "We gotta do something. Maybe we still got time."

"I suppose, if we can get hold of the cops quick."

"What do we do with her, Carter? We can't leave her here."

"Gimme a sec."

Carter went over to Fiona, still standing motionless in the corner. He put his hand on her shoulder. She flinched, and he pulled his hand back like he'd touched a hotplate.

"Fiona. We need to get out of here."

She didn't say anything, but turned to face him. Tears were dripping down both cheeks. She made no attempt to wipe them away. He made a tentative move to touch her face. She didn't try to pull away, so he brushed the tears back from one cheek and then the other. She closed her eyes for a moment. When she opened them again, they were still glistening.

"You know we have to try to stop them," said Carter.

She nodded.

"If we find a policeman right away, or a phone, maybe they can keep them from setting off that bomb."

When she finally spoke, her voice trembled. "B-b-but where are they going?"

"I know where," said Carter. "At least the name of the place. Somewhere called Burlington Arcade. You know where it is?"

Fiona shook her head. "I've heard of it. Somewhere on the West End, but I've never been there. It's for the fancy folk, I think."

"Well, doesn't matter. The cops'll know, and that's all that counts."

Fiona grabbed Carter's arm again. This time her fingers dug in, and Carter tried to loosen her grip. He could see streaks of her blood on his shirt as her hand slipped down. She said, "I've got to get there. Got to help Gordie. Gordie and Fergie. Got to help them."

"We'd never get there in time. But maybe the police can. Maybe. If we hurry and get to them now. The longer we wait . . ."

Fiona pulled away from Carter and started for the door. Over her shoulder she said, "You do what you have to do, but I've got to go to them. If the police stop them before they set off the bomb, I need to be there if they been arrested."

"Wait," shouted Carter. "What if you don't get there in time? What if they blow the thing before you do?"

From the doorway, Fiona said, "I can't think that way. Anyway, I still gotta be there, one way . . . or the other."

"Then I'm going with you. This time you're *not* going off on your own . . . don't look at me like that. I don't care if you think I'm treating you like a helpless . . . it's not because you're a girl, and . . . well, you are, and, and I can't stand . . . darn it, I can't say how I feel."

Josh spoke up. "I'll warn the cops. You go on, lover boy, and do what you two gotta do."

Carter and Fiona took off down the alley. "Careful of the potholes," said Fiona. "That's how I ruined my hands."

"I wondered."

At Brixton Road, they were able to speed up on good pavement. Carter said, "I know Josh said he'd call the cops, but if we see one, we stop and tell him. Right?"

"I guess."

They didn't see one. At the Stepney Green Tube Station they had to wait in line behind an older woman who had to rummage through her pocketbook looking for train fare. Practically dancing with impatience, Carter asked Fiona if she knew where they needed to go. She didn't.

Finally, they reached the ticket window, and Carter practically shouted to the attendant, "We need to go to Burlington Arcade. What station is that at?"

The ticket-seller said he didn't know. He shouted to one side, "Bernie, this fella needs to go to . . . where was it?"

"Burlington Arcade."

"Burlington Arcade, Bernie. Ya know it?"

When the answer came back from Bernie, the ticket man said, "Piccadilly Circus, mate. One way or return?"

"One way. Two tickets. And hurry."

"What's the fire, mate? Can't go till the train comes, anyway, i'n'at right?"

Carter was tempted to tell him there was something a heck of a lot worse than a fire involved, but decided that would just slow things down further and wouldn't do any good.

When the train came, after what seemed like an eternity, they leaped on and plopped into the nearest seats. As they pulled out of the station, Fiona leaned toward Carter and said, "How do we know this train goes to Piccadilly Circus?"

Carter looked stricken. "I . . . I guess we don't." He practically shouted at a woman sitting opposite them, "Piccadilly Circus. Does this stop at Piccadilly Circus?" The woman acted like Carter was threatening her and drew her hands up to her face. Carter lowered his voice and repeated the question. He even tried on a tentative smile. This time she answered, in the form of a shrug and an "I don't have a clue" gesture.

There was only one other person in the car, a young man at the far end. Carter jumped up and went to repeat his question. This time he started off with an "Excuse me."

The man said, "I don't think so. Check the map." He motioned to a map of the Underground rail system on the wall. Carter ran over and studied it, trying to find out where Piccadilly Circus was and where they were at the moment, somewhere near Stepney Green. He became aware Fiona had come up beside him.

"There's Piccadilly," he said, pointing to a dot on the map.

"And we're here," said Fiona, pointing to a place just west of the Stepney Green dot. "Oh, no! They're not on the same line. We'll have to change trains."

"It gets worse," said Carter. He pointed to Stepney Green on the map. "There's two lines go through here. If we're on the green one, that's the District Line, I think; it goes one way, and we gotta change to the brown line at the Embankment Station. If we're on the orange line, it goes way the heck up that way. Where we change trains depends which way we're going. You didn't happen to notice which train we're on, did you?"

Josh Weaver followed Carter and Fiona out into the alley. He figured he'd be right behind them but glanced to his right and saw a red telephone booth. He stopped and searched his pockets to see if he had change for a call. He did, so he took off in the opposite direction from Carter and the girl. At the corner he dragged the coins out of his pocket and pulled open the phone booth door. It made a creaking sound, and he saw the booth looked like it was a hundred years old. The walls were covered with graffiti, some of it telephone numbers, some really foul language, and some words he didn't even recognize but guessed he'd never use around his mother. The black phone was dented and scratched, and the mouthpiece hung down at the end of a spiral cord. He picked it up and listened. Silence. He waggled the cradle up and down and listened again. More dead air.

Josh threw the phone down in disgust and looked up and down the street for another phone or a store that would have one. Nothing in sight. All he could see were what seemed to be more storage buildings like the one he just came out of. *Better head back through the alley. There's stores on Brixton Road. The pastry shop'll have a phone.*

He took off on a run, dodging potholes every few feet. He didn't notice a loose stone that tilted when he stepped on it. Trying to keep his balance, his other foot slipped into a hole, and he felt himself hurtling toward the pavement. He tried to stop his fall with his hands, but his body was twisting sideways and the last thing he was aware of was the grey pavement rushing toward him and a brief flash of pain.

Old Roscoe thought the alley would be a right proper place for a nice whiz and maybe a doorway for a bit of a nap. He was leaning against the wall in mid-whiz when he noticed the form stretched out in the middle of the alley. *Blimey. That bloke never even made it to a doorway. Silly bugger.* After he'd halfway managed to fasten his trousers, he went over to the inert form and pushed it with his toe. "Bit too much of a pub crawl, mate?" The body on the pavement didn't respond, so Old Roscoe did what any self-respecting fellow would do—he bent down and started to search through the pockets of the unconscious fellow. Then he thought, *What if this bloke ain't unconscious? What if he's dead?* He shrugged. *All the less he'll need whatever spare change what's on 'im.*

Old Roscoe was a tad disappointed in his findings. One opened package of cinnamon chewing gum, a set of keys, a few shillings, and two piddly pound notes in a skinny wallet. Hardly worth the search but better than nothing. He started to walk away, but turned back and stared down at the young man on the pavement.

With a sigh, he leaned down and felt the lad's cheek. Seemed warm enough. *Since he's been kind enough to share with me, guess I'd better get him out of the middle of the road.* He pushed the lad sideways. That didn't work too well, so he went around to the other side and pulled on him, rolling him toward the wall. The last few feet he had to go back to pushing, so he used his foot. One last effort put the young man up against the wall and Old Roscoe flat on his behind. He got up and said, "Well, mate, hope you're satisfied." He started to leave, then turned back and said, "Thanks for the handout, matey. Now don't you worry none. I'll make good use of it."

By noting the names of the stations they passed and keeping an eye on the wall map, Carter learned they were on the District Line, the green line on the map. Finally some good news, as this one came way closer to Piccadilly than the orange line. They still had to change trains at the Embankment Station, but it was an easy shot to Piccadilly from there.

The Piccadilly Circus Station was a mass of people. Worse, there were exits in several directions, and there was no way to know which one to take. Again, Carter took to shouting at strangers, in hopes someone could help them find which way to go for Burlington Arcade. Finally, one man motioned to one of the exits and said, "Turn right top of the stairs, cross the street, turn right again. Half mile. Can't miss it."

Carter hoped the man was right. Of course, if there was the sound of an explosion or they saw a posse of cop cars with lights and sirens, they sure wouldn't miss it. They followed the man's directions and rushed as quickly as they could, dodging sightseers and cheerful families carrying brightly colored shopping bags. Ahead there was nothing but the same, as far as they could see. No smoke, no police cars, nothing but people going about the business of living.

Carter and Fiona jogged as fast as they could, dodging people on the sidewalk. He managed to say, "I don't understand. If it's . . . just up here, like the guy said, there oughta be . . . cops everywhere. Josh should have had plenty of time . . . to find one or call them, and they . . . should've had plenty of time to get here."

A few blocks later, Fiona grabbed Carter's arm and pulled him to a stop. "That van up there. The white one."

"Yeah?"

"It looks like the one me brothers got into back in the alley. I'm sure it is."

Before they got close, a man came running out of an opening just beyond the van, bumping into one of several rounded posts that were between the building and the street. He slapped at the post and then kicked it, before leaping into the white van and pulling out into traffic. A car had to slam on the brakes to avoid a collision, and honked the horn. A fat black taxi behind the car had to brake, too, and that horn joined in. "That was the guy called Paddy O'Brien," said Carter. "This is it, all right." They watched O'Brien pull ahead a few hundred yards, where he found another parking place and stopped.

At the spot where the agitated O'Brien had come into view, Fiona pointed above the entryway to a double row of shops. An ornate carved sign read, "Burlington Arcade." A group of women came out of the Arcade, chattering and laughing. A couple with a small child in hand was going the other way. Carter could see dozens of people strolling along inside, or gazing into store windows. One or two pointed at things on display. Everyone seemed content, even happy, at what they were doing. There was no sign of danger. No bomb. No bombers. No brothers named McKenna.

"Maybe they changed their minds," said Carter.

"But I know that lorry was the one from the alley, and I'm sure that man O'Brien was the one nearly smashed me foot drivin' it."

Carter opened his mouth to say something, then shrugged and headed into the Arcade. "C'mon. If your brothers are here, we'll find them."

Inside, with traffic noise behind them, the atmosphere was even more peaceful. Even the few young children in the crowd seemed to sense this was a place where noisy behavior was out of place. A few of the shoppers were dressed in the casual clothes marking them as tourists, probably American. Most, though, were dressed in fine clothes that matched the quality of those displayed in the windows. A man dressed in an old-fashioned top-hat and tails strolled through the crowd, nodding his head and tipping his hat to everyone who passed. *Weird*, thought Carter. A jewelry store had just a few pieces artfully displayed on draped black velvet. A china shop's wares were back-lit so you could see how thin and translucent the dinnerware was.

Carter began to breathe easier, when Fiona gasped and said, "There they are. Gordie and Fergie. In there." She pointed into a shop displaying vases and other gifts in the window. "What are they doing?"

She started inside but found the door had been closed and locked. Fiona raised her fist to rap on the glass, but Carter grabbed her hand and said, "Wait. Let's watch for a minute and see." What they saw provided almost no new information. The two brothers were in the far back of the shop, behind a display counter. They stared at the floor, not moving.

While Fiona and Carter were watching, a man came up behind them and muttered, "Women! Said she'd be here, now she's off who-knows-where. Like I've got all bloody day to hunt her down." He went off with his arms crossed and his head tilted so he could check out each shop along the way.

Carter said, "I don't have a clue what they're up to. Might as well go in. I'll knock. Your hand's a little beat up."

Fergie looked like the Loch Ness Monster had climbed up on shore and introduced himself. He rushed to the door and said, "Fiona. What the devil? And . . ." to Carter, ". . . you! How'd you get away?"

"Thank your sister for that."

"You gotta get out of here, Fiona. Now."

"I'm not goin' nowhere till I knows what you're about. You been sneakin' off for days, and me and Mum . . . I got something to tell you about Mum."

Fergie looked anxiously down the Arcade and then back at Gordie, who seemed to be frozen in the back of the shop. "We ain't got time for that, now. You just get out, you hear?"

Fiona put her hands on her hips. "You don't tell me what to do, Fergus McKenna." She held her hand up, showing Fergie the blood-red scratches. "I went to a lot of trouble to find you. What I found was me own flesh and blood tied up my friend here . . ." She pointed at Carter. ". . . and I still don't know anything about what you're up to. So don't . . ."

"Too late!" Fergie stared behind the trio at the gift shop door. Carter turned and saw the man called Haverty striding toward them. He had one hand in a jacket pocket, and it was thrust out toward the front. Carter had seen enough gangster movies to know there might or might not be a gun in Haverty's pocket.

Haverty seemed to read his mind. "You don't know if there's really cold steel in me hand, do you? Thinking of taking a chance and running? You might consider the consequences of guessing wrong. On you, and your pretty little girlfriend here."

Carter looked at the bulge in Haverty's jacket and shrugged.

Haverty said, "Seems I'm always escorting you through doorways, doesn't it? Well, don't let me disappoint you. Go on in." He motioned with the bulge in his pocket.

Fiona and Carter filed into the gift shop, followed by Haverty. Fergie locked the door behind them. Gordie kept shifting his eyes between his sister and the floor behind the counter. He seemed scared and, something else, thought Carter. *Ashamed maybe.* Carter was really frightened himself, but decided it would be a good idea to try and hide it. He said, "Hello, Gordie. How's it going? Aren't you glad I brought your sister by to see you?"

The effect on Gordon McKenna was more than Carter had expected. Fiona's twin brother swiveled his head toward a closed door in the back of the shop and didn't move for a moment. When he turned back there were tears streaming down his cheeks.

"Gor blast it," Haverty yelled. "I knew little brother was gonna be the weak link in the chain. You get him under control, Fergie, or we got a real mess."

"He'll be fine," said Fergie. "Won't you, Gordie?"

Gordie nodded. He didn't say a thing but went back to staring at the floor. By this time, Carter had edged back to where he had a clear view of the thing that had Fergie's attention. What he saw was the body of a middle-aged woman, dressed in a dark blue suit and a white scarf that had come partly loose and was framing a face twisted in terror. Something red had been stuffed into the woman's mouth, and it was fastened in place by a piece of grey tape, the same tape that was used to bind her hands and feet.

"Shouldn't we get her into the back room?" said Fergie. "With the shop fellow?"

"No reason to," said Haverty. "Won't make no difference to her now, will it? What we got planned here is gonna make sure there ain't no difference where either of them is." He pointed to one of the three boxes sitting next to the terrified woman.

Carter looked at Fiona to see how she was taking this. Her eyes were fixed on Gordie, and she barely gave the box a glance. *She doesn't know. Doesn't have a clue that's a box full of death.* Death for that woman on the floor, death for whoever was in the back room, death for the innocent people walking by in the Arcade. And if Carter was correct, Haverty meant for that fate to include Fiona and himself. He tensed to spring at Haverty but hesitated just a moment when he saw the gun, a real one after all, pointed straight at him.

Haverty said, "Don't even think about it."

Chapter 23

"It's pretty sure," said Carter, "you're planning to blow us up. If you shoot me, I won't end up any more dead."

"If I shoot you, do ya think it'll be a nice clean head shot? Bam, and it's all over?"

"I . . . I don't . . ."

"Let me help. If I shoot you, it'll be a lovely gut shot. Right there through your nice little belly button. Maybe a tad lower. You'll be in more pain than you ever thought possible. And you'll feel the life pouring out a big ugly hole right there in the middle of you. You'll be beggin' for that bomb to go off. When it does, it will be the sweetest thing in the world to you. So, you wanna be the big, brave man and rush me? C'mon, give it a try."

Fiona was still staring hard at the woman on the floor. Then she jerked her head up, with a puzzled look mixed with terror. "Bomb?"

Still holding the gun, Haverty grabbed Fiona's arm and pulled her behind the counter. Carter was just at the point of taking the risk of getting shot in the stomach, but Haverty pushed Fiona and told her to get herself down next to the nice lady. "You, too, lad," he said to Carter. "You have a good lie-down, too."

From off the counter, Haverty took a roll of duct tape and handed it to Fergie. "Do up this bloke same as the old woman. I don't have nothin' to stuff in his mouth, so just run a couple a strips of tape across and around their heads. We only needs to keep 'em quiet for eight minutes." After Carter was bound with hands behind his back, and gagged, *again!*, Fergie told Haverty he wasn't about to tie his sister up and leave her here. He helped Fiona stand.

"Not to worry, I'll take her with me when I go. She'll be just fine." Haverty looked at his watch and shook his head. "I saw O'Brien down the street and told him to have the van back out front in exactly twenty minutes. Had it all planned just right till these two showed up. You go out and find him, tell him to stall an extra ten minutes. Not sooner and not a minute later, you got it? We'll be comin' out that door acting like we don't got a care in the world, but that van better be there, or else."

"I'll go," said Gordon. "I'll find Paddy. And I can take Fiona, too, so's she won't get in your way."

"I don't think so, Gordie, lad. I think I'd best have you with me." To Fergie, he said, "Okay. Now get going. And remember ten extra minutes, not nine, not eleven."

As soon as Fergie had gone, he handed Gordie the gun and said, "You keep 'em in your sights, ya hear?"

Gordie took the gun as if it were scalding hot. "I . . . I . . . I never held a gun before. Not in me life. I don't know . . ."

"You'll know what to do if either of these two makes a move. You'll know. Now I gotta set the timer." He opened the box with the bomb and fiddled inside for a minute or two. Carter was frantically trying to communicate with Gordie, but all he could manage was to shake his head and try to plead with his eyes. Gordie shook his own head and muttered something inaudible before he turned his face away. Carter wasn't sure but thought Gordie had said, "I'm sorry."

Haverty stood and brushed his hands on the sides of his clothes. "Well, Gordie, lad, that's it. Eight minutes till showtime. But first, hand me back the gun. I need you to check the storage room to make sure the shopkeeper's still tied up nice."

"What?"

"Just do it, lad. And, little lady, you go with him. Don't want you runnin' off when me back is turned."

Gordie had opened the door to the back room, but he turned back and said, "I can't do this, Haverty. I just can't."

"Just check on the store man. No big deal."

"I mean all of it, what we're doing. The bomb. Everything."

"Little late for that now, Gordie. In seven minutes, it's done." Haverty grabbed Fiona by the arm and thrust her at Gordie in the doorway. Gordie fell backward with his sister on top of him, and saw Haverty swing the door closed. As he did so, he said, "This is all for the better, Gordo."

Gordon McKenna had never thought of himself as quick, or strong, but now he felt an adrenaline surge that had him thrusting Fiona aside and plunging like crazy for the closing door. One more second and it would be shut. Two more and the lock would be turned. He crashed into the door and shoved himself against the wood. He felt it give way so suddenly, he barreled through and landed on the floor.

Haverty stood to one side and watched young McKenna sprawled in front of him. Calmly, he reversed the gun in hand and brought the butt down on Gordie's skull. Then, with Fiona screaming and running for her brother, he shoved the door closed in her face and turned the lock. He permitted himself a little smile of satisfaction as he calmly strolled out the door of the shop. He checked his watch. Six minutes. Perfect. Couldn't possibly be better.

Chapter 24

Carter had stopped thrashing and now felt an odd calmness. He should still be fighting against the tape that bound him, but he knew it was of no use. He'd heard Haverty lock the shop door on his way out. No one was coming. Even if he managed to roll himself to a place where passersby could see him, what would happen? They couldn't get in the locked door, and he knew if one of them ran for help, there would be a dozen others, maybe more, lined up at the glass windows watching him. *They won't know they're lining up for their own execution.* Five minutes. Maybe less now.

He thought of Fiona in the back room. The faint shouting he could hear through the door had stopped. He worm-crawled his way past Gordie's inert body and stared up at the door. Yes! The key was sticking out of the lock, but it was several feet over his head. He pulled himself into a sitting position and kicked sideways until he'd brought his back to the door. Now the hard part. He pushed with his fists against the floor to lift his butt a couple of inches. Then he pushed with his feet, trying to force his way higher. It didn't seem to be working, and he yelled in frustration. Then he realized by rocking his torso back and forth, he could inch his way upwards. *Centimeter my way upwards is more like it.* Still, little by little he raised himself, until finally he could fold his feet underneath and then stand.

Now he had to locate the key and manage to turn it, no easy thing behind his back. He had the horrible vision of dropping the key and having to crawl back down on the floor and repeat the process of getting himself up. Luckily, he located the key and would have shouted for joy when he felt it turn in the lock, if his mouth weren't taped shut.

Fiona gasped when she saw Gordie still motionless on the floor. She hugged Carter and gasped again when she noticed the tape still hobbling his legs and binding his head and arms. She started to work on the tapes covering his mouth, but he turned his back and shook his arms to show her he needed his hands freed first. When they were loose, he worked on untaping his feet. Finally, he got to the tape wrapped twice around his head. He couldn't help but groan in pain as he pulled it from the back of his head, bringing some hair with it. Worse was ripping it off his face. He hadn't shaved in days, and there was enough stubble to make it feel like he was being skinned.

"C'mon," he shouted at Fiona, grabbing her hand and pulling her past Gordie and toward the front door. "We only got a couple of minutes."

"No!" She pulled away from Carter and ran back to Gordie, who hadn't moved an inch since he went down. "I'm not goin' without me brother." She started to pull on Gordie's legs, but he was too heavy for her.

Carter said, "Oh, man, this is crazy," as he left the front door and ran back to help her. Gordie's dead weight was flopping around on the floor, and Carter's fingers, numb again from the tape, kept slipping. "We're not gonna make it, Fiona. You get out of here. Now!"

Fiona cried, "Not without Gordie. If he dies here, I don't want . . . I won't care about meself."

Carter dropped Gordie's legs and rubbed his face. *What would they do in the movies?* He ran to the brown cardboard box and pulled back the flaps. There it was, half-packed with rows and rows of dull red cylinders. On top was what looked like a metal baking tray, and on top of that were several wires leading to a battery and others down into an opening in the stack of dynamite. What caught Carter's attention, though, was a small black box with a clock face on the front and two wires going into the back. The timer. Set to go off any minute now. *Or any second. Who knows?*

In the movies the hero always has to decide whether to cut the red wire or the blue wire, because cutting the wrong one would set off the bomb. But here there was no red wire, or blue wire. *All* the wires were grey. *No sense worrying about which is the right one. If I get it wrong, that's that. But if I don't even try and head for the door, I'd probably run out of time and not make it anyways.* He looked at Fiona and decided there was no way he'd even try to run if he could, and leave her here with her brother. No way. Not to mention the woman on the floor and the shopkeeper.

The battery. To keep the bomb from blowing, the best thing he could think of was to unhook the battery. It needs a spark to set off the dynamite, doesn't it? Carter took a deep breath and froze. He could feel the seconds ticking away as he held two innocuous-looking grey wires in his hands. How could anything so simple mean the difference between life and death? He knew every second might be the one that could make all this indecision meaningless. There was no other way. He had to act and act now. He gripped one of the wires tight with a hand still numb enough to feel nothing. He closed his eyes and pulled with all the strength he had in him.

Chapter 25

WHEN THE TELEPHONE RANG AT the Chamberlain home, it was Nelda Chamberlain herself who answered. Maddie Westfall was on her way to the kitchen to prepare an afternoon tea, but the tone in Nelda's voice made her stop and listen.

"Yes, this is she. . . . No, no, start again, you're calling from where?" Nelda sucked in her breath. She held the phone with both hands while she listened. Maddie turned back and sat on the sofa next to Nelda, who held a hand over the speaker and told Maddie in a hushed, quavering voice, "It's the police, the London police!"

After another half-minute listening to the voice on the phone, Nelda said, "Yes, of course I've heard the news. It's horrible. But what has that to do with my Carter? . . . Oh, God, no." Nelda Chamberlain took in a deep breath and looked to the ceiling.

Maddie was beside herself, sitting by and listening to this conversation. "What is it? Please, is he hurt? Is Carter all right?"

Nelda held up a hand to silence Maddie. Babs Kroome came into the room and started to say something. This time it was Maddie who raised a hand in warning. After another minute, Nelda said, "Yes, I understand. I mean I *don't* understand, why he was there. It makes no sense. . . . Well, thank you for calling. Yes, yes, I will." She hung up the phone and stared at a spot on the wall where there was nothing to see.

Then the tears began to flow, and she reached for Maddie, who edged her way closer. She clung to the older woman and said, through her tears, "I was so scared. The police. Do you have children, Mrs.?. . ."

"Maddie. Call me Maddie. And yes, I have one daughter, but she's quite grown now and lives in Newcastle."

Nelda continued to stare at the wall. "That's nice."

Babs spoke up. "I can't stand not knowing. What did the police say?"

"They said the strangest thing. They said, in addition to the two bombs that went off in Hyde Park and Regents Park today, there was a third bomb, in a place called Burlington Arcade. They said my Carter was there, with that girl, Fiona."

"Noooo. He wasn't? . . ."

"No, he wasn't killed or hurt. The bomb didn't even go off."

"Thank goodness," said Maddie. "But then, there's one thing I don't understand. Why, if he wasn't hurt, would they call you?"

"Because, they said something I really can't understand, they said Carter was some kind of hero. Said he, what word did they use? Defused the bomb. Saved the lives of maybe dozens of people. I don't understand any of it. It doesn't make sense."

Maddie took hold of Nelda Chamberlain's hand and said, "It makes perfect sense. I don't know why he was in Burlington Arcade, but I know it's in his nature to take risks to help others."

Nelda Chamberlain gave Maddie a quizzical look. "What are you saying?"

"The first time I laid eyes on Carter was on a train from London. Some rowdy, and quite intoxicated, soccer hooligans were harassing a girl Carter had never before met. At some considerable risk to himself, your son pulled that young lady to safety."

"Fiona."

"Quite so," said Maddie Westfall.

Nelda Chamberlain started to cry again, and Maddie put an arm around her. Nelda didn't pull away. Maddie said, "You can be very proud of the boy you raised, you know?"

"That's just it. All these things you're telling me about him, I *didn't* know. And what happened today . . ."

"You'll have plenty of time to get to know your son again, my dear. Now, how about that afternoon tea?"

After the Storm

*M*ADELEINE WESTFALL AND BEVERLY Kroome spent many afternoons with Nelda Chamberlain, who quit cussing at them and finally came to depend on them. She really hated to leave "the girls" when it came time to move back to the United States, but after the divorce, there would really be no excuse to remain in England.

Crista Cordelia Piper found it both a necessity and a joy to spend her afternoons with Meara McKenna, whose own happiness at regaining her full mind was tempered by the plight of her two sons. After the Chamberlains had moved away, Maddie, Babs, and C.C. resumed their habit of downing a pint or two of shandy at the *Cock and Crow* several times a week. Meara McKenna was made a full partner in their little club.

Richard Chamberlain was promoted to European Regional Manager of Sales for his company. He was confident this would give him ample salary to provide alimony and child support, with enough left over to entertain a secretary. Or two.

Paddy O'Brien and Fergus McKenna were arrested and sentenced to five years in prison for their aborted attempt to blow up Burlington Arcade. Gordon McKenna was given probation without jail time, as his brother testified Gordy was "way too stupid" to be an active part of the conspiracy. Gordy got a job mucking out horse stables, much to the delight of his twin sister, Fiona.

The man known as "Haverty" disappeared. The British authorities decided if he were ever caught, it would be under another name and for another crime. Pity.

Josh Weaver never got his camping trip. He did, however, bear a scar on his forehead, thanks to the trip he took in a pothole-filled alley. All the girls at ASL said it made him look "mysterious." He felt that would be a real asset in later life, when he became a world-class detective.

Carter Chamberlain felt like the most unlucky person on earth. Sure, it was a blast being interviewed for the *Guardian* and photographed outside Burlington Arcade with Fiona on his arm and throngs of people crowding around and telling him how heroic he'd been. But the very next day, his mother announced they were moving back to the United States. She'd decided on Colorado because Gwen was there, and she wanted all three of her children nearby. "Without Maddie and Babs, I'll need you all to keep me out of trouble," she said. Carter begged to be allowed to stay in England until he'd finished his senior year in high school, but was told that was impossible.

A week after moving into their new home in Boulder, Colorado, Carter got a pastel green letter in the mail, postmarked *London, England*. It read:

Dear Carter,
  I can't tell you how lonely I've been with you gone. I tell myself it's for the best, because you have your family and I have mine, but still. . . .
  I'm going back to school this fall to finish up my A-levels, and then it's on to veterinary school. For some strange reason, I have it in my mind I want to care for horses. Two or three of the horses that were injured but not killed in Hyde Park that day got sent to a

farm outside London. I would give anything to be one of the people caring for those beautiful creatures and giving them love.

Here's the hardest part of this letter, Carter. I know you're going to be with all sort of new friends there in Colorado during your last year in high school, and then it's on to university. It doesn't seem right for you to be wasting away your time thinking of an Irish girl halfway around the world. So, please, Carter, think of yourself, meet other boys—and girls—and have a wonderful life.
Your friend,
Fiona

Carter threw the letter on the kitchen table, banged his fist a few times, and grabbed the letter up again. He started to rip it into strips, but stopped himself halfway through the first tear. He smoothed the letter on the table, folded it carefully and put it back into the envelope. *Not this time, Carter. Not this time.*

Author's Note

On the 20th of July, 1982, the author traveled by train from his suburban home in Rickmansworth, England, to downtown London. This was the daily commute to his office in a building a block south of Hyde Park. At work that afternoon, his daily routine was interrupted by a thunderous sound. Rushing to the window, he saw a plume of smoke rising from the direction of the park. There had obviously been an explosion.

He and his workmates knew something horrendous had happened, but he didn't realize the full horror of the event until he got home and watched the excited newsmen on television. The blast he witnessed was from a large nail bomb hidden in a blue car parked along the edge of Hyde Park. It was detonated, probably remotely, just as a troop of the Household Cavalry, the Queen's official bodyguard regiment, passed on their daily ride to Buckingham Palace and the changing of the guard ceremony. Three soldiers were killed instantly, and a fourth died later. Many tourists who had assembled to watch the parade were injured by flying nails and other shrapnel. Almost as disturbing to the animal-loving British, seven of the regiment's horses were killed outright or had to be put down due to their injuries.

Shortly afterwards, a second bomb exploded under the bandstand in nearby Regent's Park during the performance of the music from *Oliver!* by the Royal Green Jackets military band. The crowd in attendance was peppered by shrapnel, causing dozens of severe injuries. The entire band was either killed or injured by the blast.

These two very real tragedies were the inspiration for this book. There was no aborted third bombing in the Burlington Arcade. That is an entirely fictitious invention of the author, as are every one of *Windstorm*'s characters, even the bombers. In the real world, a man named Gilbert (Danny) McNamee was arrested five years later for the two park bombings. He never admitted his guilt. He was released from prison in 1998, and a judge overturned his conviction because of withheld fingerprint evidence that implicated other bomb-makers.

—Ted Simmons

Author Bio

Ted spent most of his career as a technology manager for a major oil company, mostly in international producing operations. This gave him the opportunity to live and travel in some of the world's most fascinating places. He developed a keen interest in the cultures and beliefs of other peoples, and believes many Americans would benefit from some of his insights.

He lived in the jungles of Sumatra, the deserts of Kuwait, and traveled extensively in such far-flung places as China, Egypt, Vietnam, and the various countries in the Middle East (Uzbekistan, Kazakhstan, Azerbaijan, Turkmenistan).

During the 1980s, Ted and his family lived in the suburbs of London, and he worked in a downtown office building just a few blocks from a horrendous act of terrorism perpetrated by the Irish Republican Army. This experience was the inspiration for the actions and characters in his novel *Windstorm*, young and old. As in all his stories, the main characters, Carter Chamberlain and Fiona McKenna, are beset with troubles at multiple levels, some external and some that they carry around in their own hearts.

LaVergne, TN USA
30 April 2010
181095LV00005B/12/P